TEMPT ME *With* DIAMONDS

JANE FEATHER

ZEBRA BOOKS
KENSINGTON PUBLISHING CORP.
www.kensingtonbooks.com

ZEBRA BOOKS are published by

Kensington Publishing Corp.
119 West 40th Street
New York, NY 10018

All Kensington titles, imprints, and distributed lines are available at special quantity discounts for bulk purchases for sales promotion, premiums, fund-raising, educational, or institutional use.

Special book excerpts or customized printings can also be created to fit specific needs. For details, write or phone the office of the Kensington Sales Manager: Attn.: Sales Department. Kensington Publishing Corp., 119 West 40th Street, New York, NY 10018. Phone: 1-800-221-2647.

Zebra and the Z logo Reg. U.S. Pat. & TM Off.

First Printing: February 2019
ISBN-13: 978-1-4201-4360-7
ISBN-10: 1-4201-4360-3

ISBN-13: 978-1-4201-4361-4 (eBook)
ISBN-10: 1-4201-4361-1 (eBook)

10 9 8 7 6 5 4 3 2 1

Printed in the United States of America

"DAMMIT, RUPERT. PUT ME DOWN."

She pushed against his chest, but his hold merely tightened.

"No," he said calmly, heading up the stairs. "Not yet. I'm enjoying the feel of you." He shouldn't be teasing her, Rupert knew, not when she was so vulnerable, but somehow he couldn't help himself, and besides, it was perfectly true.

"Oh, you're insufferable." It was more than she could bear and she grabbed at his ear, twisting hard.

"Vixen," he said appreciatively, turning along the gallery to her bedroom. Shifting her in his arms, he turned the knob and pushed the door open. The velvet curtains were drawn and the gas lamps were lit but turned down to provide a soft light. The coverlet on the bed was folded over, and on the dresser stood a small Primus stove, a saucepan of milk, a cup, and a plate of sweet biscuits.

"Very inviting," he observed, carrying her over to the bed. "Would you please let go of my ear now?"

Diana's fingers opened, releasing his earlobe. She looked up at him, at his face bent so close to hers. An arrested expression crossed his countenance, and she was suddenly very still in his arms, a soft flush warming her complexion, her gaze holding his before fixing upon his lips, hovering just above hers.

Imperatively, she lifted her hands to grasp his face and brought his mouth down to meet hers.

Also by Jane Feather

Love's Charade

Smuggler's Lady

Beloved Enemy

Reckless Seduction

Chapter One

London, August 1902

Rupert Lacey, as was his habit, moved from sleep to wakefulness in a matter of seconds. He opened his eyes abruptly, aware of the faint gray light of dawn showing between a gap in the curtains and the unmistakable sense that something was happening in the house. There was nothing specific to give him this feeling, no particular sound, just a stirring of the air, a sense of motion. He sat up, reaching for the bellpull on the wall beside him.

It was answered within minutes. Davis, his batman, came into the bedroom carrying a tea tray. "Good morning, Colonel." He set the tray by the bed and went to draw back the curtains.

"Seems we have a visitor, sir," Davis continued, imperturbable as always. "Miss Sommerville arrived a short while ago . . . with her household, it appears."

"Oh, did she indeed?" Rupert took a fortifying gulp of the strong morning brew that his years in

South Africa had made a morning necessity, swung his long legs out of bed and rose to his feet. He slept naked as always, another habit acquired during the hot African summer nights. He stood for a moment, holding his teacup with one hand, stroking his chin with the other. Then he drained his cup and said briskly, "Pass me my dressing gown, Davis?" He would have preferred to greet Diana fully dressed but there was no time now for such niceties.

He had wondered how she was going to react, and when. He had expected her to bring the fight to him one way or another. Diana had never been able to resist a challenge or a battle of wills.

But what if her arrival had nothing to do with the will? What if she didn't know about the will as yet? Dear God, he hoped she did. Either way, all hell was about to break loose.

He shrugged into the robe Davis held for him and made for the door, tying the belt securely. He stepped out onto the wide gallery that ran along either side of the horseshoe staircase that rose from the marble-floored hall of the elegant Cavendish Square mansion. He hung back in the shadows for a moment, looking down into the hall at the invasion below.

Steamer trunks and hatboxes were piled high, and in the midst of them Diana Sommerville stood, stripping off her gloves, issuing crisp orders to two servants. On either side of her sat two magnificent South African Ridgebacks, the original lion hunters. They appeared placid enough, gazing around them with their sharp, intelligent eyes, their long, sleekly muscled bodies poised for instant movement.

"Barlow, would you organize the library and yellow parlor for my immediate use? I doubt we'll have callers for a few days, but just in case, we should have the drawing room fit for visitors as soon as possible. Mrs. Harris, would you go to the kitchen and create order there? I expect it will take some work to put the house to rights again." A dazzling, conspiratorial smile accompanied her words, and the two retainers returned the smile with understanding nods.

"I'll have it all back to normal in no time, ma'am," Mrs. Harris declared. "I daresay the Trimballs have done their best to keep the house in good shape, but . . ." She gave an eloquent shrug. Caretakers could not be expected to keep an empty house up to snuff. "Come, Izzy, I shall need your help if Mr. Barlow can do without you for the moment." She swept away in her black bombazine dress, a small parlormaid trotting at her heels.

Rupert hadn't known how he would react when he saw her again, but now he knew that nothing had changed. He had wanted to punish her for the hurt and disappointment she had inflicted upon him, but all he could see now was that Diana was as wonderful as ever, and he responded as ever to the imperious, arrogant set of her small head, the richly luxuriant coffee-colored hair curled fashionably into a fat chignon at the nape of her long neck, the tall, slender frame that seemed to throb with energy, the pleats in her rich silk skirt moving gently, hinting at the restlessness of the long legs beneath. Such wonderful legs. For a moment, he was distracted by a memory of her naked body hovering above him, her legs scissoring his thighs.

He stepped forward out of the shadows. "Good morning, Diana." He rested his elbows on the gilded railing as he looked down.

Diana Sommerville's head jerked upward. She stared at the figure standing on the galleried landing. "*You?* What in the devil's name are you doing in my house?" Her eyes were purple fire, her complexion ashen as she stared in bewildered fury at the man she had hoped never to encounter again. He was wearing a brocade dressing gown, the tie accentuating the slim waist and his copper curls fell in that familiar, unruly tangle on his brow.

He had just got out of bed. In her *house.* It made no sense. He couldn't possibly be here, the man she had sworn never to speak to again. And yet he was. Just as if time had slipped away and it was as it always had been in the days when Rupert Lacey was as welcome on Sommerville property as the Sommerville children themselves.

"Get out," she demanded. "*Now.*" But to her frustrated bewilderment, she could hear the futility of the demand. She was no physical match for him, and if he wouldn't go, she couldn't wrestle him out of the door. But why was he here?

Rupert cursed silently. So she didn't know what had happened. How the hell was he to handle this?

"I said, get out of my house," Diana repeated, ignoring the sense of futility even as she wondered why he wasn't saying anything. If anything, he looked vaguely discomfited, not an expression she would ordinarily associate with Colonel Lacey.

"I have no idea how you got in, or why you're here, but you are trespassing."

Rupert sighed. Explaining this situation to Diana in full combat mode was not something he wanted to do. "As it happens, Diana, I am not trespassing. I assume you have not yet visited Muldoon?"

"Muldoon? The solicitor?" She looked even more bemused. "What has he to do with your breaking and entering my house?"

"A great deal, as it happens," he said dryly, beginning to descend the stairs. "Not that I did either of those things."

The two dogs, who had been sitting alert but quiet at Diana's heels, growled in unison, a deep and threatening sound.

Rupert blinked in surprise. He and the dogs were old friends. Nevertheless, he took a step back to the gallery. Diana's hostility was enough to provoke their instincts to defend her even against someone they had known since they were puppies.

Diana laid a hand on each dog's head, saying softly, "Hera, Hercules." They subsided, but their eyes never left Rupert and the muscles rippled beneath their sleek coats, their long bodies still very much on the alert.

Rupert decided to take the coward's way out and let a professional handle the situation. Sometimes discretion was indeed the better part of valor. "When did you arrive in England, Diana?"

"Yesterday evening, as it happens. But I fail to see what that has to do with your illegal presence in my house." Her eyes challenged him in a way that was achingly familiar, but he resisted his usual response to meet and match the challenge. This was neither the time nor the occasion for the old ways. There'd be opportunity enough later, he was sure of it.

"Muldoon will explain it to you, Diana. I suggest you visit him at once. I know you won't listen to me, but you will listen to him."

Diana turned away from him, her gaze sweeping the mountain of luggage as if somehow its very presence could make sense of this impossible, unbelievable situation. Her butler and personal maid were trying not to look fascinated by the scene being played out before them. They had known Colonel Lacey since he was a lad at boarding school with a penchant for mischievous adventures. And they knew the present state of affairs between Miss Sommerville and the colonel.

Diana made up her mind. She couldn't unravel this craziness alone, and if Muldoon could offer some kind of explanation, she needed to hear it at once. She hated to leave the house with Rupert still in possession, but it seemed the only way, because he clearly had no intention of going anywhere. "Barlow, would you see if the hackney is still outside?"

The butler bowed and hurried to the still-open door. Two hackney carriages stood at the door. Both drivers were wrestling with the last few pieces of baggage fastened on the roofs. "Still here, Miss Diana. Still unloading." He stepped aside as one of the men staggered past with a heavy steamer trunk, setting it down with a sigh of relief.

"Then please tell one of the cabbies I need to be taken to Chancery Lane."

"Right, ma'am." He turned back to the still-open front door and sent a piercing whistle through the early morning air. "One of you needs to take Miss Sommerville on to Chancery Lane."

"Should I accompany you, Miss Diana?" asked a thin, angular woman, who had been standing to one side, her sharp gaze moving between her mistress and the man on the gallery as if she were watching a tennis match.

"No, thank you, Agnes," Diana replied. She didn't need a chaperone, and her personal maid had better things to do in the next hour. Resolutely, she kept her back to Rupert, as if by ignoring him she could convince herself he wasn't there. "Would you see to the unpacking? I'd like to settle in as soon as possible."

"Indeed, ma'am. Izzy can help me once Mrs. Harris doesn't need her."

Diana nodded, drawing on her gloves again. She felt very strange, disoriented, bewildered and not really in control of anything, however much she tried to give an impression of imperturbable command. Muldoon, the family solicitor, would restore that control. He'd make damn sure Rupert Lacey left her house in short order.

"The cabbie's ready, ma'am."

"Thank you, Barlow." She inhaled deeply and walked to the open door, her head high and back straight, telling herself that she was not leaving Rupert in possession of the field. When she returned she would come armed.

Chapter Two

Half an hour later, Diana stepped out of the hackney carriage on Chancery Lane and stood for a moment savoring the soft warmth of the English summer morning as she gathered her thoughts. It was still early, barely nine o'clock, but she had been so anxious to get installed in Cavendish Square that she'd left Brown's Hotel, where she'd spent the previous night, after her arrival on the White Star liner from South Africa at soon after seven thirty. It had been the beginning of the South African winter when she'd left Cape Town for the monthlong voyage home, the dawn mornings bitter when she'd ridden out to watch Kimberley Diamond training on the racetrack. The cold air had seemed to suit the racehorse. How would the filly respond to her new home in the English countryside?

But there were more pressing matters at the moment than the well-being of a racehorse, however important she was. Diana walked up the shallow steps to the front door where a brass plate proclaimed the offices of Messrs. Muldoon and Muldoon, Esq., Solicitors. She pressed the bell and the door was opened almost immediately by an elderly frock-coat clad clerk.

He blinked in surprise at his unexpected visitor. "Why, Miss Sommerville, how delightful to see you. We didn't realize you were back in the country. A letter was sent to you in South Africa only last month."

"I had left by then," she said, managing a slightly shaky smile. "I arrived in Portsmouth only yesterday, Mr. Bates. Would it be possible for me to see Mr. Muldoon?"

"Yes, yes, of course. I'll tell him you're here. He'll be so pleased to see you." The clerk held the door wide. "Please, step inside, Miss Sommerville."

"Thank you." She stepped past him into the cramped foyer from which rose a narrow flight of stairs. The air was stuffy and smelled dusty, a smell she remembered from past visits to the family lawyers. An attic smell of ancient books and piles of parchment. It was oddly comforting in its familiarity, as was Mr. Muldoon, who came hurrying down the stairs, rosy-cheeked and rotund as ever. He bowed with old-fashioned courtesy and kissed her hand.

"My dear Miss Sommerville . . . Diana . . . I wrote to you just last month. I wish I had known you were coming home."

"After my father's death so soon after my brother's, I found it difficult to stay in South Africa." She smiled the same shaky little smile.

"Yes, yes, I understand." His clasp on her hand tightened. "I cannot tell you how sorry we are, both at Sir Geoffrey's death and at your brother's. To die so young, fighting for his country, such a brave and honorable death, but I know that can't really be a comfort."

"Not really, no," she agreed. Her anger rose again with the upsurge of grief, never far from the surface these days. "Pointless to die in a war over diamonds and gold."

Mr. Muldoon inclined his head in acknowledgment but after a pause said with a slight note of reproof, "Those gold and diamond mines, Diana, are responsible for your family's considerable wealth."

Diana flushed with annoyance. The solicitor was presuming on the years of his firm's service to the Sommerville family. She said sharply, "Maybe so, Mr. Muldoon, but my brother's life was not worth that fortune, however pleasant it is to possess it."

The solicitor reared back, like a tortoise withdrawing his head. He'd forgotten about the Sommerville eyes, the deep purple of sloes. Alight with that flash of anger, they burned like purple fireworks.

Diana instantly regretted her spark of temper. She had to watch her tongue; it had always been her downfall . . . speaking her mind without a tactful pause, that vital moment of reflection. Jem had had a similar problem, but he controlled the impulse better than his younger sister. Rupert, of course, had never pulled his punches, except when it was in his interests to do so. But of course, Rupert Lacey was not a Sommerville, for all that he acted as if he were.

Which brought her to the point of this visit. But before she could say anything further, Muldoon said, "I'm very glad to see you, my dear. As you would not have received my letter with a full explanation of your circumstances, I must explain matters to you in person. Please come into my office."

Diana felt the first tremors of apprehension. Her circumstances were surely perfectly straightforward. She followed him into a dusty chamber, littered with papers and books, its paned windows grimy with the city's heavy air, thick with the stench of sea coal and the smoke from the barges plying the river. She took the chair he pulled out for her and waited as he took a thick file of papers from a drawer in an over-flowing cabinet and sat down on the opposite side of the big desk.

He spent a few minutes riffling the papers, pat-ting them into alignment, before finally folding his hands on top of the pile and regarding Diana gravely through his pince-nez. Her apprehension now was running riot as she waited, breathless, for him to speak.

"As you're aware, Diana, your father, Sir Geoffrey Sommerville, stipulated that upon the death of himself and Lady Sommerville, his estate be divided equally between your brother, Jeremy, and yourself. The estate comprises Deerfield Court and its lands and home farm in Kent, the London house on Caven-dish Square and the property, gold and diamond mines in Kimberley, South Africa."

He paused, and Diana looked at him expectantly. "Yes indeed, I understand that, Mr. Muldoon. And because my brother predeceased our father, the entire estate now passes to me. Is that not so?"

The solicitor cleared his throat. "It's not quite so simple, I'm afraid."

Something monstrous was beginning to take shape in Diana's head. She sat bolt upright, her gaze fixed upon him. "How so? Jem had no heirs."

"Your brother, Jeremy Sommerville, made his own will, leaving his half of the estate to Colonel Rupert Lacey, a close friend from childhood and a fellow officer, I understand."

And the monster was now roaring, fully formed. She was white as a ghost, her eyes strangely blank as she stared at him, for a moment unable to speak.

Muldoon looked at her anxiously. "Can I get you a glass of water? Perhaps a cup of tea . . ."

Diana declined with a gesture, her hand pressed to her lips as she gazed blankly into space. "It's not possible," she murmured, so softly he could barely hear her. "It's not possible that Jem would do that to me." She shook her head vigorously. "You must be mistaken, Mr. Muldoon." But she knew he was not. Muldoon did not make mistakes, and certainly none of this magnitude. And Rupert had warned her, after all, although he hadn't had the courage to tell her himself.

"I'm afraid not, my dear." He slid a sheet of paper from the pile across the desk to her. "This is a copy of your brother's will. It is signed and witnessed, quite incontestable."

Diana picked it up with nerveless fingers and forced herself to read it carefully. And then she read it again. It was in Jem's handwriting and it was signed by him and witnessed by two of his fellow officers. Jem was nothing if not thorough when he set his mind to something. But *why* would he do this? Oh, she knew he and Rupert were close, and remained so even after the debacle between his sister and his best friend, but never in her worst imaginings could she have believed he would betray her in such a fashion. Half of everything, even Kimberley Diamond, the racehorse they had bought together, trained, whose racing career they had planned. Their joint project over which brother and sister had spent hours of time together.

She handed the paper back. "Nothing can be done?"

He shook his head. "Of course, you might be able to come to some amicable negotiated agreement with Colonel Lacey . . . a division of the various properties, or perhaps the sale of some of them and a division of the proceeds. I would be more than happy to facilitate such negotiations and draw up the necessary agreements. In any way I can be of service, my dear. I have served the Sommerville family for over twenty years."

Diana stood up and moved toward the door. Her voice was a monotone as she said, "Thank you. I need to think. I'll come back to you when I've decided what to do."

The solicitor followed her down the narrow staircase and opened the front door, standing aside as she stepped past him into the warm sunlight. The hackney stood waiting for her at the curb. Mr. Muldoon hurried to open the door for her, and with a distracted nod, Diana stepped up into the gloomy interior.

The cabbie leaned down. "Back to Cavendish Square, ma'am?"

"Yes, thank you." She held out her hand to Muldoon. "I'll be in touch when I've had time to consider my options."

He bowed his head in acknowledgment, closed the door and stepped back as the cabbie shook the reins and the horses moved forward.

Diana sat back against the cracked leather squabs, vaguely aware that her hands were shaking. She glanced at her watch and was surprised to see it was only ten o'clock. It felt as if she'd lived through a whole week in the few short hours since she'd woken at dawn in Brown's Hotel on Dover Street. She peered through the grimy window, looking out at the busy streets, so different from the peaceful, lush landscape of the veldt, the long, shimmering reach of the Orange River, so different from the noisy, crowded, gray expanse of the Thames, snaking its way through the city.

The unconnected thought pierced her dim trance that fashions had changed since she was last in London. She wondered if it was possible for life at some point to assume a sense of normality again so that she could contemplate a shopping trip with her friends. She hadn't seen Petra and Fenella since their debutante season had ended two years ago and she'd sailed to her family in South Africa, secretly engaged to Colonel Rupert Lacey. They were to be married in Cape Town, while he and her brother, Jem, served with the army, protecting the English gold and diamond mines against the Boers. When

the war was finally won they would return to England
and take up married life.

Diana sat bolt upright on the narrow seat. How
could she ever have felt such passionate love for a
man who was now anathema to her? It was a question that had haunted her since she had discovered
his deceit. She had challenged him to deny it, and
he hadn't done so. And again she felt that sharp,
cold stab of betrayal. For a moment, she thought
she could smell the scent of the veldt on the breeze
coming off the Orange River, feel the heat of the
sun on the back of her neck that afternoon, when
she had tossed him the question, her tone light-
hearted, her belief in his love and loyalty absolute.
And he had simply looked at her, unsmiling,
something strange lurking in his clear green eyes,
which were as penetrating as ever, and after a long
moment he had shrugged, as if it were a matter of
supreme unimportance and turned away, leaving
her standing on the riverbank, as if she too were a
matter of supreme unimportance.

The cab turned onto Cavendish Square and
drew up once more outside the Sommerville
house. Except that it wasn't just the Sommerville house anymore. Half of it belonged to Rupert
Lacey. But they could not both be under the same
roof. Rupert must see that. Society would be scan-
dalized. Not that she gave tuppence for that, but she
couldn't possibly endure such proximity and surely
neither could he?

She opened the door and sprang lightly to the
ground, feeling in her reticule for the fare. Once
she was properly installed, she would need at least

two footmen, who would monitor the front door and deal with paying cabbies and taking in parcels and greeting visitors.

She could buy Rupert out. She could afford to. And the house didn't have the same meaning and significance for him as it did for her. Of course, that was the answer. The absolute rationality of the solution brought a surge of positive energy.

She looked up at the house, thinking it looked blind, motionless, as if in waiting. The elderly Trimballs, caretakers responsible for ensuring the roof didn't leak, the chimneys were swept and rats didn't run rampant over the kitchen and scullery, had been its only occupants among the dust sheets since her last visit.

Jem had been there on that visit too. The house without her brother was going to feel so strange, and some of her hopeful energy faded. She remembered it as it was when she was a debutante, when Jem was a young dragoon filling it with his fellow soldiers. An army of servants moved with discreet efficiency, seeing to every need of their employers, expressed or not. But since Jem's death at Mafeking, everything she did, everywhere she went, accentuated the rawness of his absence.

She climbed the steps to the front door, lifting the bronze lion's head door knocker and letting it fall with a clang. Barlow opened it instantly, the dogs at his heels, greeting her with ecstatic tails. She glanced around the hall. There was no sign of Rupert and she breathed a sigh of relief. Short-lived, however.

"Ah, you're back." He stood in the doorway of the breakfast room. "How did it go with Muldoon?"

She regarded him coldly. He was dressed in uniform, the scarlet jacket accentuating his broad shoulders, the tight britches his slim hips. *Why did she have to notice his physique?* She didn't want to notice him at all, let alone with the little quiver of remembered lust she could not deny.

"How do you think it went?" Her eyes were purple ice chips, her voice frigid.

It was not a question that expected an answer. Rupert shook his head slightly. "You'll have to forgive me, Diana. Your sudden arrival has me at something of a loss. Unfortunately, it is neither unexpected nor pleasant, but it does leave me rather short of stimulating conversation."

"Really?" The delicate curve of her dark eyebrows lifted in mockery.

"If you wish for breakfast, I'll leave you in possession of the table." He gestured to the room behind him. "I can recommend the kippers."

"Oddly, I find I have no appetite. Now, if you'll excuse me." She turned on her heel toward the stairs, the hounds falling in on either side of her.

Rupert moved forward swiftly, standing at the foot of the stairs, not blocking her way but presenting an obstacle. "Diana, there is no way out of this. Let us please try to make a civilized arrangement. I am willing to compromise to a certain extent, and if you do the same, then we might brush through this without spilling blood."

Diana laughed, a delicate peal that contained nothing but scorn. "You were always too sure of yourself, Rupert. As it happens, Mr. Muldoon pointed out several solutions. Now, if you'll excuse me . . ." She gathered up her skirt and moved past him up the stairs, leaving the faint scent of orange blossom on the air.

Rupert watched her mount the stairs, a slight frown drawing his straight brows together. If she wanted a fight, he would give her one. But what *solution* did she have in mind? Oh, well, he decided, he'd find out soon enough. He returned to his kippers.

Chapter Three

Diana entered her bedchamber, the dogs beside her. She closed the double doors behind her and leaned against them for a moment, trying to restore her composure. She was going to achieve nothing if every encounter with Rupert was so antagonistic that rational discourse was impossible.

Agnes turned from the wardrobe, where she was smoothing the folds of a gown she had just hung up. "Ah, there you are." She regarded her mistress shrewdly. She had taken care of both Diana and Jem in the nursery. During Diana's years at boarding school, she had looked after Lady Sommerville, both in England and South Africa, and on that lady's death had simply transferred her attentions to her daughter. Lady Sommerville's death had coincided with the end of Diana's schooling, so it had seemed an obvious move. She had steered Diana through her debutante season rather more effectively than her aunt, who had taken responsibility for her now-motherless niece's come-out.

"You haven't eaten anything this morning," she now stated, taking in the young woman's pallor. "Izzy, go down to the kitchen and bring up a pot of coffee, toast and two boiled eggs."

The girl was on her knees in front of an open steamer trunk. "Right away, Miss Agnes." She struggled to her feet and hurried to the door, dropping Diana a bobbed curtsy as she left.

"I'm not really hungry, Agnes," Diana demurred, though without conviction as she knew her words would have no effect on her old nursemaid.

"You will be soon enough," Agnes said, continuing with her work of unpacking. "All this gallivanting around at this time of the morning. I don't know what things are coming to. What her ladyship would say, I really don't know."

Diana rightly assumed the latter muttered comments included Rupert's surprising presence as well as her own breakfastless morning. She sat down on the broad cushioned window seat and kicked off her shoes, curling and stretching her stockinged toes, letting the room settle around her. There was something wonderfully soothing in the familiarity of her own bedchamber. It had always been a haven, the soft blue wallpaper, the cream velvet curtains, the gold silk coverlet on her wide feather bed, the blue and gold Axminster carpet underfoot. Her father had talked about bringing the new electric light into the house, but he had died before he could fulfill his wish, and Diana was not sorry. She liked the soft warmth of gaslight, but at some point, she would have to yield to progress.

Izzy came back struggling under a laden tray,

which she set down on a small table beside the window. "Mrs. Trimball made apple jelly from the apples in the garden," she said. "For the toast. Should I pour the coffee, ma'am?"

"Please." Diana shifted from the window seat to a chair beside the table. She found to her surprise that she was actually hungry. Hera and Hercules stretched out with deep sighs, their heads resting heavily on her feet. She sliced the top off the first egg, sprinkled the revealed yolk liberally with salt and dipped the tiny silver spoon into the creamy golden interior.

She felt that surge of positive energy returning with each swallow of coffee. Rupert was the first order of business. Once that was sorted out, and here she resolutely pushed down the impossible idea that it wouldn't be sorted out, she would start living life again. She had written to Fenella and Petra from South Africa, telling them her sailing dates and when she expected to be in residence in the town house again. She would write today and tell them she had arrived. If they were in town, they would visit immediately, she knew. Her spirits lifted anew at the prospect of having her friends with her. And then she would have to discuss with Barlow and Mrs. Harris the servants they would need to hire to bring the household to full strength. She, herself, would not need to be involved in the hiring; the housekeeper and butler would know much better than she what they wanted in a member of staff.

Was Davis, Rupert's batman, in residence as well as his colonel? He would be, of course. Rupert was still in the army and Davis's loyalty to Colonel Lacey was unquestioned.

A light tap at the door brought her reverie to a close. Izzy jumped up and went to the door. "Colonel Lacey requests the pleasure of Miss Sommerville's company in the library at her earliest convenience," Barlow announced, his voice expressionless.

Oh, he was going to have to wait, Diana thought grimly. Her earliest convenience was going to be several hours away. He could pace the floor and twiddle his thumbs waiting for that moment.

"Inform the colonel that I have received the message, Barlow," she said coolly.

"Very well, ma'am." The butler's lips twitched a fraction. He had witnessed many a squabble between young Rupert Lacey and Miss Diana over the years. Master Jem had usually refereed the arguments. But things were very different now. Barlow's flicker of amusement died. He closed the door and went to deliver his message.

Rupert was in the library, which struck him as the most neutral room in the house. The Trimballs had been set to remove the dust covers, sweep and polish, while Diana had been with the solicitor, and the room felt lived in again. He was standing at the long French doors that opened onto the small walled garden at the rear of the house when Barlow delivered his message. His lips tightened; so, she was going to play games.

"Please inform Miss Sommerville that I have appointments at Horse Guards. I'll not return until midafternoon. I trust she will be available then."

"Very well, Colonel." Barlow bowed.

"Oh, and, Barlow, would you ask Davis to send to the mews for my horse, please?"

The butler bowed and stepped out of the library. It seemed that for the moment he was serving two masters. He went in search of the batman.

The urge to go upstairs and have it out with Diana was difficult to resist, and Rupert caught himself stalking to the door, choice words upon his lips, when he stopped himself. If he indulged the urge, she would have the upper hand. And that was not going to happen. He had let down his guard with her before, something he had learned as a small child never to do with anyone, and she had almost destroyed him. She wouldn't get the chance to do it again.

In her bedroom, Diana slowly finished her breakfast. "I think I'll change my dress, Agnes. It feels as if I've been wearing this for a week."

"Will you be going out again, Miss Diana?"

"No. I have letters to write and must discuss various domestic arrangements with Mrs. Harris and Barlow. I want to get the house back to normal as soon as possible."

"Something light and comfortable, then," Agnes declared, examining the contents of the wardrobe. "This, I think." She shook out the folds of a simple muslin dress. "It won't require a corset if you don't wish to wear one within doors."

But would it provide sufficient armor for facing Rupert, which she was going to have to do later today, when she'd made him wait long enough? But he'd seen her in a lot less, considerably less, Diana reminded herself. She couldn't erase those memories from his mind, so it mattered little, and the last thing she could face right now was whalebone and tight laces. For some reason, she had the idea that a lack of physical constraint would make it easier to duel with Rupert, would make her mind nimbler.

That shouldn't make sense, but it did. "The dress is just right, Agnes."

Half an hour later, she went downstairs to the library. Barlow had given her Rupert's message, so she was not expecting to find him. She had her meeting with Mrs. Harris and Barlow, wrote to her aunt in Albemarle Street, knowing that any delay would be seen by that lady as gross negligence and wrote to Fenella and Petra, hoping they were in town.

She sealed the letters, gave them to Barlow to post and then sat back among the thick leather cushions of a sofa and closed her eyes. It had been a long and stressful day and she was suddenly tired. It was warm in the library with the afternoon sun pouring in. A fly buzzed drowsily against the window and sleep beckoned, her eyelids drooping.

Chapter Four

Rupert stepped quietly into the library and trod across to the sofa. He stood looking down at Diana as she slept. A slight smile touched his mouth. She looked so serene, as if nothing could disturb her tranquility. Her mouth was soft and relaxed, those fiercely beautiful eyes hidden beneath paper-thin lids, the long lashes dark half-moons against the creamy complexion. Her mother had been a renowned beauty in her day, and her daughter had inherited that beauty. She had not, however, inherited Lady Sommerville's temperament, he reflected with a flicker of rueful amusement. Diana's mother had been the epitome of calm serenity. Nothing discomposed her. She sailed through the tempestuous waters of life with her volatile husband with quiet composure, and Sir Geoffrey had adored her for it.

Diana had inherited her father's temperament with her mother's beauty, and it made for a fascinating if wild ride for those who closely inhabited her world. And most particularly for those fortunate, or perhaps unfortunate, enough to love her.

Diana opened her eyes, and for a moment looked up at him with a slightly puzzled expression, as if she didn't know where she was. A smile trembled on her lips and then abruptly disappeared as full awareness returned. She sat up abruptly, swinging her legs off the sofa so that she was sitting upright again. He took a step backward to put some distance between them.

"Nice sleep?" he asked easily, as if the tension between them wasn't stretched taut as a tight rope.

"It's been a tiring day," she responded with heavy irony.

"I'm sure." He retreated to the empty grate and stood with one arm stretched along the mantel, one booted foot on the brass fender. A picture of relaxation. "Where would you like to start?"

Diana still felt the residue of sleep cobwebbing her mind, making clarity of thought difficult, and she needed to have her wits about her for this. She leaned back against the sofa cushions, resting her head, looking at him thoughtfully. "How did you do it, Rupert?" The question sounded merely curious.

"Do what?"

"Oh, come on, you know full well what I mean. How in *hell* did you persuade Jem to do it? To betray me?" The edge in her voice was now sharp enough to cut.

"What makes you think I did anything, Diana?"

She sat bolt upright again, her eyes shooting that purple fire at him. "Because he never would have betrayed me without coercion. What did you do?"

For a moment, Rupert struggled to control the flood of angry words that hovered on the tip of his tongue. She'd accused him of dishonor once before and now she was doing it again.

"I did nothing," he stated flatly. "And you impugn both my honor and your brother's with such an accusation. Jem was his own man, and you know that perfectly well."

"He never would have done something to hurt me if he had had a choice," she shot back at him. "So I have to conclude that for some reason he had no choice. And because you appear to be the beneficiary, and I know the influence you used to have with him, I ask again, *what did you do to get him to leave you his inheritance?*" Feeling at a disadvantage, she stood up, the thin muslin gown settling around her. She was tall, and Rupert had only a couple of inches on her, so that their eyes were almost on a level when she faced him directly.

Rupert took a deep, calming breath. She was goading him to lose his temper, something he was well used to. He had known her since she was the adored eight-year-old sister of his closest school friend. A sometimes-annoying adjunct to their activities, but an amusing companion when it suited them to include her. Until she changed. How well he remembered that first school holiday when she had come back to Deerfield Court with her hair no longer hanging in a thick plait but piled fashionably on top of her head, revealing the white column of her neck. Her skirts now skimmed her ankles and the grubby scratched knees of childhood were a thing of the past.

But she was as spirited as ever, up for any challenge, and during the tempestuous years since that summer, he had wavered between indulging himself by taking up her challenges and trying to resist her provocations. He didn't succeed often in the latter response. Usually, the temptation was too great. However, on this occasion, given the shock of her morning's discovery, her angry questions were probably understandable, for all the insulting presumptions they were based upon. He certainly had no intention of answering them. Not yet anyway. Only when, or rather if, he thought she would be receptive to the truth.

"As I've said, Jem was his own master. I'm surprised you would question that, because you share the same stubborn self-will," he stated with a dismissive gesture. "But this is the situation, and while I can quite understand your position, could we try to be civil and find a way to live with it?"

Diana was silent for a moment. He had a point, and if she wanted him to accept the solution Muldoon had given her, she would achieve nothing by forcing a full-scale war between them. "Yes, you're right," she said pacifically.

He smiled. "That must have cost you something, my dear. No, forgive me." He held up his hands in a gesture of peace as the fury lit her eyes again. "I couldn't resist it, but it was truly ungenerous of me. Please, let's start again."

They had so much history, Diana thought . . . so much passion running beneath the years of their relationship, passion both good and bad. She closed her eyes briefly, then said, "Very well. Ring for Barlow, will you? I would like a glass of sherry."

He obliged, and when the butler appeared asked him to bring the sherry decanter. Barlow glanced swiftly between the two of them. "Right away, sir. Mrs. Harris would like to know if you will both be in for dinner and what time you would like it served."

"I'll have dinner on a tray in my room, thank you, Barlow," Diana said swiftly. Whatever détente they might achieve in the next hour, she could not imagine breaking bread together.

"I'll be dining at my club," Rupert said.

Barlow bowed and retreated. Silence reigned in the library until he returned with the sherry decanter and two glasses. "The pantry is somewhat bare, Miss Diana, so I'm afraid there are no biscuits to accompany the sherry. But Mrs. Harris and Mrs. Trimball are making a list for Fortnum's, and Billy, the Trimballs' boy, will go to fetch the hamper later."

"Yes, good, thank you," Diana responded somewhat distractedly. She couldn't think of domestic matters at this point. She took the glass the butler handed her and sipped the golden liquid. It seemed to bolster her flagging energy, and once Barlow had left, she said briskly, "There's a way around this impossible situation, Rupert, so let's discuss it."

"Willingly," he responded, watching her over the lip of his glass. "Not that I consider the situation impossible, myself."

"Well, of course it is," she said impatiently. "Two unmarried people under the same roof? Think of the scandal. And Aunt Tabitha will fall into a convulsion."

He laughed. "Since when have you given a damn

for convention and scandal, my dear? But for the sake of appearances, I suggest we let it be assumed we were married in South Africa. As I understood it from Jem, our engagement was not a very well-kept secret, although it was never formally announced. Jem also told me that you chose not to inform your friends and relations, those people who were in on the secret, that you had broken off our engagement. Or did you have second thoughts?"

Diana stared at him, dumbfounded by the truth. To all intents and purposes, as far as people close to her were concerned, including Aunt Tabitha, she had left for South Africa a year and a half ago secretly engaged to Rupert Lacey. And she had simply neglected to tell anyone at home that the marriage hadn't taken place. A monthlong sea voyage had separated her from the people at home, and that dreadful afternoon had left her as raw as if she had lost a skin. She couldn't face revisiting it by writing to anyone immediately, thinking that if and when she went home there would be sufficient distance from the emotional devastation of her broken engagement to make it easy to shrug it off in casual conversation.

Her father's health had been declining and he had little interest in the world around him unless it was directly related to the war and his Kimberley gold and diamond mines. Jem had gone to fight the Boers, to protect the family's mining interests, leaving her alone to care for their increasingly irascible, ailing parent. She had done the only thing possible by pushing her personal miseries to the back of her mind while she concentrated on caring for her father.

Her brother's death at Mafeking had been the last straw for Sir Geoffrey. His health had gone downhill rapidly and she had nursed him to the end. The last time she had seen Rupert had been at her father's funeral. Sir Geoffrey had been a surrogate father to him since he was twelve, but he had kept himself away from Diana, staying in the background and leaving as soon as the ceremony was over.

And she had barely noticed his presence or his departure. Jem's death and then her father's had obliterated whatever pain she still felt at Rupert's deception. *Until now.*

"Have *you* told anyone?"

He shook his head. "No. It wasn't necessary, as I hadn't told any of my fellow officers of our engagement in the first place."

"No one at all?" she asked with a strange stab of wounded pride. "Wasn't it news worth sharing?"

"I have always preferred to keep my business to myself," he responded with a slight shrug. "Once the wedding took place, they would have learned of it soon enough. But then . . ." He gave another dismissive shrug and let the sentence die.

Diana was silent, sipping her sherry. He was right to say she couldn't care less about scandal, particularly now, when there was no one close to her to be hurt by it. If she had chosen to share her house with Rupert Lacey, she wouldn't have given a second thought to the inevitable whisperings. *But she hadn't.* The issue was moot anyway, because they were not going to be living under the same roof.

"So . . . your solution to a problem I don't believe exists?" he prompted.

"It's Muldoon's solution, actually, to the problem that I cannot under any circumstances endure even the idea of sharing a roof with you." Diana walked to the French doors leading to the back garden. She sipped her sherry, keeping her back to him. If she wanted to avoid distraction, it seemed safer. She was too quick to react to his reactions and she wanted to keep her head clear.

"I am willing to buy you out and you would then be able to buy your own town residence. That would satisfy your need for a townhome," she continued in a rush.

Rupert appeared to consider this as he kept his eyes on her back. He could see the points of her shoulder blades under the thin muslin and detect the rigidity of her slender shoulders. Her back was as eloquent as her face to one who knew her body as he did.

"No," he said flatly. "That would not suit me at all."

She spun around at that. "*Why* not? It's what you want, isn't it? A townhome. I'm offering it to you on a plate. Muldoon will make all the legal arrangements."

Rupert shook his head. "But I want *this* house, Diana. Or at least half of it."

"But that is so unreasonable," she cried.

"I don't see it that way. Jem gave it to me, he had his reasons and I would feel ungrateful in refusing his gift."

Diana regarded him in frustration. "He gifted you the value of half the house. Not the actual bricks and mortar."

"And how can you be sure of that, Diana?" He

turned aside to refill his glass, raising the decanter in offering to Diana.

She held out her now-empty glass and he refilled it. "Of course I'm sure," she declared. "Jem wasn't out of his senses. He could never have intended this idiocy. If he wanted to make you rich—and I suppose I can see that he might; you were after all his best friend and you didn't have two farthings to rub together . . ."

"*Enough.*" Rupert interrupted her harshly. "My finances or lack thereof are no concern of yours and never have been. I am sick to death of your insults. One more such remark and I shall really lose my temper."

She remembered how touchy he had always been about his impecunious state. She and Jem had always trod softly around the subject, and now she had just thrown it in his face. She would get nowhere on this track. "I'm sorry," she said. And she meant it.

He said nothing for a moment, before giving a quick shake of his head, as if ridding himself of an unwelcome thought. "Truce, Diana?"

She nodded. "Truce." It would be a temporary one, she decided grimly, but now was not the time for the full-on, knock-down, drag-out fight she was spoiling for.

Rupert regarded her with narrowed eyes. He could read her like a book. When the time was right, he would give her the fight she wanted, but now was not that time. "Very well. Now hear me out, please."

She gave a resigned shrug. "Go on, then."

He drained his sherry glass and set it down. "Which rooms in the house do you want to be exclusively yours?"

Diana exhaled noisily. "I have told you, I will not share this house with you."

"Then where do you propose going? To Deerfield?"

"*No*, I will not be forced out of my own house," she exclaimed.

"Impasse, then," he remarked, folding his arms as he regarded her with an air of exaggerated patience.

She wanted to weep with frustration, but she wouldn't give him the satisfaction. "*Why* won't you be reasonable, Rupert? If you won't let me buy you out, will you agree to sell this house and split the proceeds? Then we could each buy our own residences."

"That strikes me as a lot of unnecessary work for no proper end. Forgive me, but you're the one being unreasonable. We are joint owners of a property more than large enough for two people to inhabit independently. So let us divide the living quarters in a fair and reasonable fashion so that we can achieve that end."

There was no moving him. It was pointless to continue this until she'd had time to think up another strategy. Muldoon had made it clear there were no legal ways to undo her brother's will. She could, of course, buy herself another property and leave Rupert in sole possession, but the injustice of such a prospect was unthinkable. This house was in her blood. She had spent at least half her life under its roof.

Rupert watched every step of her struggle on her face and took the initiative when he sensed she was nearing acceptance. He stepped forward and took her hand. "Come and sit down and we'll do this properly."

His touch electrified her skin, and she started as if burned. His clasp tightened, and his green eyes were fixed upon her face with an intensity that brought a tide of memories to flood her senses. Her gaze was held fast with his, where a question lurked. It was not a question she could answer even though her treacherous body was shouting her response, and she knew her expression had for an instant been open, unguarded.

She jerked her hand free and stalked to the library table at the back of the room. "Let's get this over with." Her voice sounded different to her ears, harsh and yet uncertain. She pulled out a chair and sat down.

Rupert took a chair across the table from her. He drew a sheet of blank paper toward him and, dipping a pen in the inkwell, began a rough map of the interior of the house.

Chapter Five

"So, this is what we have." Rupert turned the paper around and slid it across the table to Diana. "As you can see, I've already marked the common areas. You mark the rooms that will be exclusively yours."

Diana examined the map. "I have to have the drawing room. You've marked it as shared . . . and the dining room. I have to have that too."

"I might have need of both, but I accept that you'll probably use them more than I will, so I suggest we leave it that when I see a need for either I'll check with you first."

"What if we clash?"

"Oh, from past experience, I'm sure we will, my dear," he responded with a grin. "But there is such a thing as compromise."

Diana swallowed. When had she last seen that wicked little grin? In another lifetime, it seemed. But it had always sent a hot jolt of lust to her belly, and it still seemed to have that power. Her thighs were quivery beneath her muslin skirt and she was glad to be sitting down.

She kept her eyes on the map before her and forced herself to concentrate. For the moment, the appearance of acceptance seemed to be the only sensible option. "I'll have the yellow salon, my mother's parlor, my own bedroom, that goes without saying, and the small breakfast room. You can have the main breakfast room and the library." She gestured to the book-lined walls around her. "That should suit you for whatever social life you intend to have."

"You're too kind," he retorted.

"Well, you already have your bedchamber. I assume you're using Jem's old room? Or have you appropriated my father's apartments?" Her voice was sharp.

He shook his head. "No, but you're right that I am using Jem's."

"I haven't seen Davis. I presume he's with you."

"Yes, at present he's walking the hounds in Hyde Park. Your maid said they were getting restless at being cooped up all day."

"Oh, dear." All the fight went out of her as fatigue and guilt swamped her. "I haven't given them a second thought all day with all this . . ." She waved an arm in an eloquent gesture.

"All this," Rupert agreed. "One last detail and then I suggest we call it a day. I'm more than happy to leave the management of the household in your capable hands, but we will share the expenses equally. Agreed?"

Diana put her face in her hands, rubbing her

eyes wearily. "I don't know . . . I need to think about it and I can't think clearly any more today."

Rupert felt an unexpected stab of guilt. He was entirely responsible for her exhaustion, although Diana, as usual, hadn't done herself any favors by fighting a lost battle so fiercely. "Very well. We'll continue this tomorrow." He stood up and went to open the door for her as she got to her feet.

She passed him, then stopped in the hall and turned back. "You're not having anything to do with Kimberley Diamond, Rupert."

He raised his eyebrows. "No? But half of the horse definitely belongs to me, the will stipulates that, and I should remind you that I am every bit as qualified as Jem was to partner with you on her training and her racing career."

Diana's eyes snapped with anger. "I beg to differ," she stated frigidly, then strode to the staircase before he could respond.

Rupert resisted the temptation to go after her. He'd had enough for one day and Diana certainly had. They would reenter the lists tomorrow.

Diana continued swiftly up the stairs. Maybe it was true that Rupert would make a good partner. He was a superb horseman and understood the needs and demands of a racehorse. But he was no substitute for Jem at her side. And it was *not* going to happen, even if she had to sell the filly to ensure it.

And that would be cutting off her nose to spite her face. The recognition did not improve her temper.

* * *

She slept soundly that night, contrary to her expectations, and when she awoke early the next morning found herself feeling much more positive. There had to be a way to win this standoff with Rupert. She pulled the bell for Agnes, who appeared quickly with her morning tea.

"Looks like another beautiful day, Miss Diana," Agnes said, setting down the tray and turning aside to draw back the cream velvet curtains. "Mrs. Harris would like to meet with you after your breakfast to talk about menus. I'll tell Izzy to fetch up breakfast immediately, and Billy will walk the dogs." She clicked her fingers at Hera and Hercules, who had risen languidly from the rug at the foot of Diana's bed and were stretching their long, lean bodies.

"Thank you, Agnes." Diana sipped her tea. "I'll get up in ten minutes."

"Right you are, ma'am." Agnes left, the dogs racing ahead of her.

Diana leaned back against her pillows, teacup in hand, and thought about the day ahead. She felt energized, her blood flowing swiftly, her fatigue of the previous evening a thing of the past. A strategy had come to her in her sleep, or so it seemed. She would quite simply ignore Rupert's presence. Just because he insisted on being there didn't mean she had to acknowledge him. She would set up her own household for her sole use. If Rupert wanted to hire servants, he was welcome to do so, but her butler, housekeeper, footmen, cook, parlormaids, scullery maids would not serve the interloper.

She would lay out the facts in writing this morning

and have Barlow deliver the fait accompli to him.
She would pay for her own household, he could do
whatever he wished. Sam, the coachman, had served
the Sommerville family for almost thirty years. If he
was ready to be pensioned off, she could manage
well enough using hackneys around town, but if, as
she suspected, he was not ready to retire, she would
keep the brougham that had belonged to her father
for her personal use in town. Her own riding horse,
Merry, had crossed the seas with her and was stabled
in the mews, with the groom who had always looked
after her. There was room for Rupert's horse and
groom, but they were of no concern of hers.

As for Kimberley Diamond . . . the filly had gone
directly from the ship with Ben, her groom and
favored companion, to the stables at Deerfield
Court. She would move to a training facility when
she'd recovered from the voyage. But if Diana had
her moved without Rupert's knowledge . . .

A slight smile lingered on her lips as she set aside
her cup and swung herself out of bed. She went to
the window and looked out over the quiet square. It
was barely eight o'clock and the streets around the
square garden were empty but for a milk cart. A
group of small boys were playing cricket in the
garden, watched over by several nursemaids. She
could hear the smack of oak on leather, a sound
that brought so many summer memories to mind.
Jem and Rupert had once played in the same way
in the same garden. Suddenly, Diana had a vivid
memory of the morning when Jem had swung
the bat with such vigor, the ball had sailed across the

railing to smash through the ground-floor window of the house next door.

Fortunately, both Sir Geoffrey and Lord Carlton, whose window it was, were passionate cricketers and considered the speed and power of the shot well worth the cost of a new pane of glass. Diana blinked back the sudden tears and turned away from the day's brightness.

Izzy's appearance with the breakfast tray provided a welcome distraction from haunting memory. "There's three letters come for you, ma'am." Izzy set down the tray on the small table beside the empty grate.

"Thank you." Diana took the envelopes. She recognized her aunt's writing on the top one and set it aside for later. The other two brought a surge of pleasure. One was addressed in the flamboyant script of the Honorable Fenella Grantley, the other in Petra Rutherford's untidy scrawl.

Her friends were both in London, then. Diana frowned suddenly as she took a sip of fragrant coffee. How was she going to explain Rupert's presence? She couldn't lie to her dearest friends. The three of them had been inseparable through five interminable years at Dovecote Academy for Young Ladies in Hampstead, a village on the northern outskirts of London. Their education there was intended to provide some academic instruction, but for the most part to turn out young ladies ready for their debutante season and the marriages that were supposed to come out of that season.

Fenella and Petra had scorned the marriage mart

process as thoroughly as Diana, but Diana had had Rupert in the wings. *Had he seduced her?* She shook her head. *No.* That first night of illicit passion had been as much her doing as his. Marriage had seemed a natural step, but because of her mother's recent death and Sir Geoffrey's subsequent retreat to his holdings in South Africa, the engagement hadn't been published in the *London Gazette* and the *Times*. A few necessary people, like Aunt Tabitha, had been told of it, and it had been assumed that the wedding would be quietly celebrated in South Africa in consideration of the family's recent bereavement. But Fenella and Petra had been her closest confidantes and had known every detail of the passionate liaison that had led to the engagement. They would be expecting Diana now to be Mrs. Rupert Lacey.

Diana spread butter and apple jelly on a piece of toast, the frown still on her brow. She couldn't hide the truth from them, but they would not betray her. It was a charade they would relish playing. And they knew Rupert of old. Sir Geoffrey and Lady Sommerville had returned to England every summer so that their children could spend the long school holiday with them either in the country at Deerfield Court or in Cavendish Square. Rupert, Jem's closest friend, was always one of the party. He had nowhere to go himself except to his guardian, a cold and distant grandfather in the Yorkshire Dales, and it became accepted that he was part of the family. Diana's friends were equally welcome, and while Jem and Rupert followed their own pursuits, as did the girls, they sat around the same dinner table, rode in

Hyde Park together on occasion and were generally comfortable in one another's company.

They would marvel at the situation, Diana knew, and would more than cheerfully enter into the spirit of the charade. So she didn't have to worry about her friends. Her aunt, on the other hand, was a different matter.

Diana speared a deviled kidney and popped it into her mouth. Was Rupert enjoying the same in the breakfast room? Who had been cooking for him? Davis, or maybe Mrs. Trimball? Not that Rupert's domestic arrangements were anything to do with her. She drained her coffee cup and went to the wardrobe, flinging open the double doors.

"So, what are you planning this morning, Miss Diana?" Agnes asked as she came into the room, the dogs at her heels. She continued to address Diana exactly as she had from her nursery days.

Diana was fingering the dark green linen folds of a plain skirt. "Household business for the most part, Agnes." She reached down to caress the dogs in turn. "I think this skirt and a white shirt blouse."

Her maid nodded. "The dark green leather belt with the silver buckle will go well with the skirt." She began to select the items from the wardrobe. "I've drawn your bath."

"Thank you, Agnes. I'll have it now." Sir Geoffrey had been one of the first to install hot water heaters and pipes in his London house, and it was a luxury appreciated by staff and family. Unfortunately, he hadn't done the same for Deerfield Court, and the servants had to labor upstairs with cans of steaming water to fill the old-fashioned bathtubs.

Diana went into the adjoining bathroom, where perfumed water steamed gently from the claw-footed tub. She stripped off her nightgown and stepped into the water, sliding down with a sigh of pleasure.

Chapter Six

Rupert read the document Barlow had brought to him in the library with increasing anger. What the *devil* was Diana playing at? What could she hope to achieve by open hostilities? She was actually suggesting they give each other a schedule of their day-by-day planned activities so they could avoid any *awkward* meetings in the house. *Awkward*. Dear God. He crumpled the paper, hurled it into the empty fireplace and strode from the library in search of Barlow.

The butler had just come through the green baize door that separated the kitchen and servants' quarters from the main house when Rupert accosted him. "Barlow, where is Miss Sommerville at this moment?" Rupert tried to master the simmering fury he could hear in his voice.

"I believe, sir, that Miss Diana is in Lady Sommerville's parlor. She asked for writing materials to be sent there."

"Thank you." The colonel accorded him a curt

nod and went up the stairs two at a time, turning at the top into the west wing. Outside the double doors leading to what had been Diana's mother's private parlor, he hesitated for a moment, then, with a muttered imprecation, raised his hand and knocked imperatively. When there was no immediate reply, he opened the doors onto a pleasant, intimate apartment that looked out onto the back garden. It had been Lady Sommerville's personal haven and bore the marks of her serene temperament in the soft rose color of its furnishings, the delicate objets d'art scattered around on carefully chosen pieces of eighteenth-century furniture.

Diana was sitting at a rosewood French escritoire and spun round in her chair, a pen still in her hand. "It's customary to wait for an invitation," she commented with icy calm.

"I see no point in wasting my time," he retorted, pushing the door shut at his back. "Do you really want to live in an armed camp, Diana?"

"Quite the opposite," she responded. "Because you insist upon staying under this roof I hope to achieve a situation where we don't ever have to engage with each other in any way at all. That was the point of my letter."

"*Letter*," he exclaimed. "You call that abominable document a *letter*?"

"Call it what you like," she said, her face very pale but her eyes full of fire. "Those are my terms."

Rupert took a step toward her, and she jumped to her feet, the better able to face him on an equal footing. Her hands were clenched into fists. "Don't you dare touch me."

"Touch you?" He looked at her, incredulous. "Why on earth do you think I would want to do that? Although," he added, "the urge to wring your neck right now is hard to resist."

Diana drove her clenched fist into his shoulder, where it met hard muscle. He seized her wrist, holding it lightly but firmly. "By God, Diana, you have a temper."

"I know that," she snapped, tugging fruitlessly at her wrist. "When you're not involved, I can govern it. But you make me lose the reins of my self-governing, and I hate you for that."

Rupert said nothing for a long moment, and his fingers circling her wrist suddenly lost their tension. "No," he said with an ironic smile. "No, you don't hate me, dear girl, any more than I hate you for the same fault. We are bound together, you and I, for better or worse. I want to fight you to the brink to break those chains, but I know they are fast and always will be. Our only hope is to find a way to live within those bonds." He dropped her wrist abruptly and turned away, back to the door.

Diana stood absently, rubbing her wrist where she could still feel his touch. The door clicked shut behind him. What had just happened? Delivered in a different tone of voice, it could almost have been a declaration of love. But it certainly wasn't that, not after everything that lay between them.

And there had been no love in his green eyes, no softness, rather a reflection of her own angry frustration. But Rupert was responsible for a situation in which she was definitely the innocent party. His frustration was his own fault. He thought he could manipulate her into accepting an appalling living arrangement. He needed to know he couldn't.

Diana pressed her fingers into her eyes for a second as she took a deep, steadying breath, then, with a dismissive shake of her head, she sat down at the escritoire again and looked blankly at the sheet of paper before her. She had been trying to frame a letter to Lady Callahan and so far had achieved only "Dear Aunt Tabitha." Her aunt would be incapable of accepting the idea of her niece living under the same roof as an unmarried man, so somehow, she had to convey to her ladyship without saying so in so many words that the expected marriage between Diana and Colonel Lacey had taken place. It infuriated her that she was obliged to accept Rupert's solution to avoid scandalizing their world, but she could see no alternative.

There was only one thing for it, she decided abruptly. She would visit her aunt before Tabitha could decide to come to Cavendish Square. Her aunt was something of a valetudinarian and, since the death of her sister, Diana's mother, had become even more so. As a result, preparing herself for a journey outside the house, even as short a distance as between Devonshire Street and Cavendish Square, was a major undertaking. If she went this afternoon, Diana decided, she would easily forestall any sudden appearance by her aunt. If she wondered why her niece's husband had not accompanied her on this courtesy call, a vague reference to military duties would satisfy her.

That settled, Diana rang for Mrs. Harris and Barlow. They would be wondering what was really going on, and it was only fair to give them some story for public consumption. Newly hired members of the household would also need to be told something that regularized the relationship between the apparent master and mistress of the house. The two old family retainers would know the truth, of course, but Diana knew they would keep their opinions to themselves and unhesitatingly present the world with the fabrication they were given. She assumed Rupert would also have taken Davis into his confidence.

However confident she was about their willingness to accept the story she was about to give them, Diana couldn't deny her awkwardness when Barlow and Mrs. Harris came in to the parlor. She was standing at the window; sitting down seemed inappropriate when she was about to ask them to lie through their teeth for her.

"Good morning," she greeted them, her smile somewhat hesitant. Then she cleared her throat and plunged. "Colonel Lacey is going to occupy some part of the house. It was my brother's wish that he be accommodated when he was in town. He will, of course, manage his own affairs, and anyone in my service will not be expected to wait upon him in any way. I understand his batman, Davis, is already taking care of him."

"That is so, Miss Diana," Barlow said without blinking an eye. "And I understand from Mrs. Trimball that he has been preparing the colonel's meals as well."

"Good, then there's nothing to concern us further," Diana said with a smile. "Colonel Lacey will

mostly use the library and the breakfast parlor if he
has guests." She paused, then, drawing a deep breath
continued. "I think it will be prudent if it is generally
assumed that the colonel and I are married."

"Of course, Miss Diana," Mrs. Harris responded,
as if it were the most obvious assumption.

"Very well, ma'am." Barlow's countenance was
inscrutable, no indication of the speculation running riot below the surface calm. He and Mrs. Harris
left, and Diana could only imagine the discussion
the two old friends would have out of her hearing.
But she also knew that no word, gossip or otherwise,
about the goings-on under a Sommerville roof
would leave the premises.

She stretched a hand to pull Hera's ears as the
dog nudged her thigh for attention. "Shall we go for
a walk, girl? Hercules, walk?"

Both dogs stood up, heads cocked, regarding her
with intelligent eyes. "I've been neglecting you. I'm
sorry." She moved to the door, the hounds ahead of
her, waiting impatiently for her to open it. She had
put on a light jacket and was crossing the hall with
the dogs bounding eagerly around her when the
doorbell rang. Her heart jumped. Not Aunt Tabitha
surely? Not yet?

She stood still, waiting, as Barlow, in his unhur-
ried fashion, opened the door.

"Fenella, Petra," she cried as two women stepped
into the hall. "Oh, it does my heart good to see you
both. I've missed you so."

"And how we've missed you, dearest," Fenella
said, her deep, resonant voice carrying as always.

"Oh, darling, we're so sorry about Jem." Petra,

tears sparking in her eyes, ran to Diana, her arms outstretched. The three women embraced, while the dogs sat by the front door with an air of patient resignation.

The friends broke apart just as Rupert came down the stairs. He paused on the bottom step, drawing on his gloves as he took in the scene. "Good morning, Fenella, Petra." His voice was calm and even.

They turned as one toward him. "Rupert, you're here . . . well, of course you are," Petra said in a rush. She hurried over to him and stood on tiptoe to kiss his cheek. He gave her a quick hug. It was impossible not to hug Petra.

Fenella held out her hand. "Rupert, it's good to see you."

He smiled and lightly brushed her fingers with his lips. "And you, Fenella." His gaze swept the hall, taking in the expectant dogs, the three women. "I am walking to Horse Guards. Lord Roberts requires my presence this morning. I can give the dogs a walk in St. James's Park, if you like, Diana, while you spend time with your friends?"

The last thing she wanted was for him to do her favors, to insinuate himself into her daily routine, and yet . . . and yet she could not have the kind of conversation she needed, longed, to have with her friends while they were walking in the park.

"Thank you," she murmured. His satisfied smile made her want to throw his offer in his face, but once again she would be cutting off her nose to spite her own face. She turned her back to him and addressed her friends. "Let's go up to my parlor. We'll have some privacy there."

She caught the quick inquiring glance Fenella cast in Petra's direction and knew that her rather stilted exchange with Rupert had not gone unnoticed. She gathered up the folds of her skirt and hurried upstairs, her friends on her heels. Once behind the doors of her mother's parlor, she gave a little sigh of relief. "It's so good to see you." She embraced them both again. "I have so much to tell you. Take off your things and I'll ring for coffee, or would you prefer sherry?"

"Coffee for the moment," Fenella said, her large gray eyes fixed upon Diana's countenance with an unnerving intensity. "I have a feeling we may be glad of the sherry later."

"No fooling you as usual, Fenella," Diana said with a rueful smile.

Fenella cast her jacket over the back of a chair and Petra shrugged out of her short cape, tossing it on top of the jacket. "I sense intrigue," she stated.

"It's not so much intrigue as a wretchedly complicated, totally unbelievable situation, and I could scream with frustration," Diana responded, pulling the bell rope by the fireplace. "Let's get coffee and I'll explain it to you."

Once Barlow had brought coffee and a plate of almond biscuits and the door had closed behind him, Petra demanded, "I'm dying of impatience, Diana. What is going on? What's happened?"

"When we last saw you, we were waving you off on a White Star liner with an engagement ring on your finger. I can't help noticing that your fingers are conspicuously bare," Fenella observed, taking an almond biscuit between her own long white fingers.

Diana poured coffee into three shallow porcelain cups and glanced at Petra, whose hazel eyes were now filled with disquiet. She was never able to hide or disguise her emotions; they were always written clearly on her face.

"I'll tell you, but it's a long and complicated story, so bear with me."

"Well, that is a pretty pickle," Fenella observed when Diana eventually fell silent. "But why would your brother do that to you?"

"And why would Rupert make it so difficult for you?" Petra added. "He's not behaving very well as far as I can see."

"No," Diana agreed. "And neither am I." It was the first time she had admitted the possibility of being even the tiniest bit in the wrong herself. Or at least the first time she had acknowledged that her main aim so far had been to ensure that whatever the situation between herself and Rupert, she would come out the winner.

"Well, what else could you do?" Petra asked. "It is your house, after all."

"Yes, and it seemed to me you made him a perfectly reasonable offer to buy him out," put in Fenella, tapping the side of her cup with an elegant manicured fingernail.

Diana smiled. It was very comforting to have such wholehearted support. "I think if it hadn't been such a shock—and I still don't know why Jem would do such a thing—then I might have handled it with a cooler head. Now, I've just created a war."

"Well, I think you had every right," Petra asserted stoutly. "After what happened. Rupert didn't even try to deny the story about the girl?"

"Or even try to explain?" Fenella added.

Diana shook her head. "No, he didn't say a word. He just looked at me, then turned and left me on the riverbank." She could still see the look he'd given her . . . startled at first, then a flicker of what for a moment she had thought was hurt, and then the pure flame of an almost incredulous anger. She'd waited for two days for him to speak, to explain, to make some kind of approach, and Rupert had maintained only an icy silence. Finally, unable to bear it another minute, she had confronted him, telling him that she had no wish to continue the engagement and had handed him back the ring. Somehow, she had expected him to protest, to offer some kind of explanation or even an apology. Rupert had merely taken the ring, bowed and wished her a good day. And, apart from a glimpse of him at her father's funeral, that was the last time she had been in his company or even heard from him until the previous day, when this whole ghastly situation had unfolded.

"But the upshot of it all is that if he won't live somewhere else, somehow we have to maintain a public charade of wedded bliss in order to avoid a scandal," she said. "And just how I'm to achieve that, I really don't have a clue."

"Well, you'd better get a ring of some sort on your finger for a start," Fenella said practically.

"Oh, it's ridiculous," she added, shaking her head. "Why would Rupert force such a charade on you? It's not reasonable."

"I wish I knew. Vengeance perhaps," Diana replied. "I broke the engagement unilaterally. Maybe his pride . . . ?" She shrugged. "Whatever the reason, unless I yield and leave, it seems he's going to insist upon this arrangement." She got up and went to ring the bell for Barlow. "It's noon. It's time for something a little stronger than coffee."

"Will you be requiring luncheon for you and your guests, Miss Diana?" Barlow inquired when he answered the summons.

Diana glanced interrogatively at her friends. "You'll stay, won't you?"

"Of course we will," Petra said. "Thank you, Barlow."

"Where would you like it served, ma'am?" He addressed Diana.

She frowned. The dining room was too big, the yellow parlor was not yet ready for use. "Is the small breakfast room set up yet?"

"Mrs. Trimball and Izzy worked on it this morning. I think you will find it satisfactory."

Diana nodded. "Good then, we'll take our luncheon there. But sherry first, please, Barlow."

"So, first things first," Fenella said. "Petra and I will support this play, of course. We'll put it about that we've seen you and that you're settling in so not up for callers just yet, which is really true. Then I suggest we have tea at Fortnum's in a couple of days and you'll see and be seen there. But first, you need to get a ring."

Diana shrugged. "That's no problem. I have plenty of my mother's to choose from. Something simple . . . she was never one for showy settings. There'll be a small diamond in her case, I'm sure. I'll have to find one before I visit Aunt Tabitha. Oh," she said with a sudden gesture of exasperation, "why would Jem put me through this? What was he thinking?"

No one spoke again while Barlow set down the sherry decanter and filled their glasses. "Mrs. Harris said luncheon will be served in half an hour, Miss Diana. Will that be satisfactory?"

"Yes, perfectly, thank you." Diana sipped her sherry.

"Perhaps Jem wasn't thinking." Petra picked up the conversation as if there'd been no pause. "After all, he wouldn't be expecting to die so soon," she continued rather tentatively. "Perhaps it was just a routine piece of business, a formality that all his fellow officers were taking care of."

That was not a totally unreasonable explanation, Diana thought. Jem was only twenty-six when he was killed at Mafeking, and he was not one to have given much thought to death and dying. Like so many of his fellow soldiers, he didn't believe they could ever lose a war against the Boers. Youth and a belief in immortality went hand in hand in those crazy days of jingoistic patriotism. He and Rupert were as close as brothers. Perhaps the possible consequences of such a will had not occurred to him. He could have seen it as a generous but obvious settlement that would not come to pass in the near future anyway. He would have assumed his sister would be married long before he faced his own mortality, even though she had disappointed him so bitterly by breaking her engagement to Rupert.

She took a sip of her sherry and felt a tiny bit less anguished at the thought that her brother had probably not intended to hurt her with his generosity. It would have been much better if that explanation had occurred to her at the beginning of this wretched business. Now she felt only remorse that she had instantly jumped to the conclusion that her brother had betrayed her.

Chapter Seven

It was midafternoon when Petra and Fenella left Cavendish Square. Rupert had still not returned with the dogs from Army headquarters at Horse Guards, and Diana contemplated a visit to Devonshire Street. She couldn't visit her aunt without a ring on her finger and started a somewhat half-hearted examination of her mother's jewelry case. The most precious gems in the Sommerville collection were held in a safe at Hoare's Bank, but the case contained a plentiful supply of more modest jewelry.

She picked out a plain silver band inset with tiny diamonds. It was discreet enough to draw little attention. She slipped it on her finger, her brow wrinkling with distaste. Not at the ring itself, but at the evidence that by wearing it she was now fully complicit in the charade Rupert had forced upon her. With a sudden gesture, she dragged the ring off her finger. Maybe she wouldn't visit Aunt Tabitha today. Surely tomorrow would do.

A brief knock at the door accompanied by an insistent whine from one of the dogs interrupted her desultory examination of the case and she rose to her feet to open the door. The dogs greeted her with wet noses and ecstatic tails. She looked over them to where Rupert stood, one hand resting on the doorframe.

"May I come in?" The question clearly didn't require an answer as he stepped into the parlor without waiting for one. "I have something for you."

"Oh?" She remained by the door, holding it slightly ajar, making clear that his presence was unwelcome.

He put his hand in his coat pocket and drew out a small tissue-wrapped package. "It occurred to me that you will need this if you're going out and about." He held out the packet.

Diana took it with a frown. "What is it?"

"Why don't you open it?"

Even as she pulled away the tissue, she realized it was a ring box. She opened it to reveal a simple, thin gold band. Not a diamond in sight, almost utilitarian, she thought. And it was perfect for this pretense. It meant nothing, carried no emotional baggage, made no declaration. She slipped it on her finger and examined her hand. "It'll do," she said.

If he was disappointed, Rupert gave no sign of it. "Good," he said. "You'd better keep it on in case you have unexpected visitors," he added as she began to slide it off.

"I have to visit Aunt Tabitha as soon as possible," Diana informed him. "Before she summons the energy to come calling."

He nodded. "Should I come with you? Lady Callahan will probably be expecting it, don't you think?"

"I'll make some excuse for you. You're needed at Horse Guards; you are after all still in the army, even though you're no longer on the battlefield." Her voice was taut, her gaze still on the ring on her hand. He was standing close to her and the proximity was unsettling. She could almost feel the heat of his body, smell the familiar scent of his skin. Somehow, she had always thought he smelled of sunshine and fresh air, even in the dusty heat of a scorching South African summer. Sometimes, when they were riding, that scent would carry the tang of fresh sweat and polished leather, and when they were skin to skin, their bodies tangled in lust, the heady scent of some kind of spice would mingle with the sweat of passion.

For a moment, the sensory memories were so powerful, she inadvertently closed her eyes, feeling her body sway a little.

"Easy." His hand came around her waist, supporting her. "What's the matter, Diana?"

She swallowed, opened her eyes and stepped swiftly away from him. "Nothing. Nothing's the matter. Or at least nothing new," she added.

He regarded her with a reflective frown. He had felt her body quiver when his hand went around her waist. He had felt his own. His own was no surprise, despite how badly she had hurt him; he had never denied his feelings for her. He would fight them to the death, but facts were facts. Diana Sommerville was under his skin.

"If you say so." He shrugged lightly. "I suggest we visit your aunt tomorrow morning and get that over with. But for now, I think we should go out this evening and have dinner at the Savoy. Let the world see us and any potential awkwardness will be over."

She looked at him in disbelief. "I am not going out with you. It's bad enough having to share a roof with you without pretending to enjoy your company in public."

"I understand, but if we do it this once, then no one will think twice in future. It's perfectly customary for married couples not to go out together. So tonight we will bite the bullet, or rather you will, my dear, and accompany me to a civilized dinner with a smile on your face."

Diana wrestled with herself. She knew he was right. They had to be seen as a couple at least once for the myth of their marriage to become a public truth. Then they could live separate lives under this roof as so many married couples did. London society was full of unhappy pairs whose marriages of convenience had outlived any pretense of liking, let alone passion.

"What time?" she asked in tacit acceptance.

"Eight o'clock. We'll take the brougham."

She gave him a curt nod and opened the door wide. "Until then."

With a sardonic half smile, he bowed. "Until then, ma'am," and walked out. She closed the door on his back with a decisive click and sat down on the chaise, playing idly with the dogs' ears in turn, while they closed their eyes with expressions of transported delight.

The last time she had dined at the Savoy had been the night before the sailing to South Africa. A large party of their friends had gathered to bid them farewell. Rupert and Jem were sailing separately with their regiment of dragoons on an army ship, headed to join the English troops fighting the Boer War. Diana remembered half-seriously suggesting they smuggle her aboard the troopship so she could sail with them.

Neither Jem nor Rupert had evinced any enthusiasm for the idea. Now she found herself smiling at the memory. They had both been somewhat shocked that she'd treated so blithely the prospect of traveling in the company of a ship full of soldiers, both officers and men. While it had been considered a great adventure by all the young men who had volunteered for the war, they made it clear they disapproved of her levity. Women were supposed to feel the war they were going to was serious business. In fact, she rather thought they'd have been pleased if she had shed a few tears at the prospect. Instead, she had been swept up in the tide of enthusiasm, the certainty that a bunch of Dutch farmers couldn't possibly outwit and outfight the cream of the British army.

She had come down to earth rapidly once on South African soil. They all had.

"There now, Miss Diana, you look lovely," Agnes declared, stepping back to survey her handiwork. "The diamonds set off the ivory gown beautifully."

Diana examined her image in the long pier glass.

Her ivory taffeta evening gown was confined at the waist with a deep rose-colored sash. She fingered the rose diamond choker circling her long neck. Rose diamond ear drops completed the picture. Agnes had worked her usual magic with the thick coffee-colored hair, piling the heavy chignon over pads on top of her head, teasing out ringlets to frame her face. She lifted the skirt of her gown and stretched out one foot, turning it this way and that. The bronze kid shoe had a high, thin heel. She liked the extra height the heel gave her. It would put her almost on a level with Rupert.

"You've achieved miracles as usual, Agnes," she said with a warm smile, holding out her wrist for Agnes to fasten the rose diamond bracelet. She felt Agnes's eyes on the thin gold band on her finger. Neither of them had referred to it during the ritual of dressing for dinner, and nothing was said now. Diana knew Barlow and Mrs. Harris would have told Agnes of the earlier discussion; they were a triumvirate of many years standing.

"Your shawl, Miss Diana." Agnes draped an Indian muslin shawl over her elbows. "The night air may have a chill when you come home."

"Now, I think I am ready." Diana drew on her white elbow-length kid gloves. "Don't wait up. I can put myself to bed."

"As you wish. I'll leave your milk and biscuits on the dresser with the Primus, in that case, should you wish to heat it up." Agnes opened the door to the gallery. "Have a lovely evening, Miss Diana."

Diana doubted that, but she smiled her thanks and stepped out onto the gallery. She could hear

Rupert's voice from the hall below. She paused at the head of the stairs. Rupert, dressed for the evening, a scarlet-lined opera cloak slung carelessly over his shoulders, was talking with his batman. Both men turned to look up at the stairs. Davis bowed. Rupert stepped to the foot of the stairs, extending his hand to Diana as she descended.

If it hadn't seemed childishly rude, she would have ignored the hand, but her earlier recognition of her own faults was enough to ensure that she let her fingers rest lightly on his palm as she stepped down to the hall. "Good evening, Davis." She greeted the batman with a cool smile.

"Ma'am. How very nice to see you again. The brougham is at the door." He walked ahead of them to open the front door.

Diana wondered where Barlow was; door opening for the mistress of the house was usually his prerogative. She glanced askance at the batman.

"Mr. Barlow, ma'am, is at his dinner. Since I shall be driving you and the colonel this evening, it seemed unnecessary for him to interrupt his meal."

Diana glanced swiftly at Rupert and he gave her a sardonic smile. *Damn the man.* He had firmly put her in her place. She could insist he had no right to use her own servants, so instead, he had manipulated her into using his. She walked out of the house, ignoring the smile, and allowed Davis to hand her into the Sommerville brougham. Rupert stepped up beside her and Davis took the box seat and picked up the reins.

It was a soft, pleasant summer night, and Diana felt herself relax. Rupert, sitting beside her, had an air of complete tranquility, looking out of the window as they drove through the busy evening streets of Mayfair. After a few minutes, he observed casually, "You look enchanting, my dear. Those magnificent rose diamonds have always suited your complexion."

"They were given to me on my twenty-first birthday," she responded.

"I know. I was there." He turned his head, giving her a smiling glance. "A night I will never forget."

She felt hot blood rush into her cheeks and turned her head sharply away from his gaze. That night had begun this whole mess. "Don't remind me," she demanded, her voice low and curt.

He laughed. "Forgive me, Diana, but nothing will be gained by denying the past. We both lived it and we both remember it."

It was true, of course. But surely he could see they gained nothing either by bringing it up all the time. Any response she would have made died on her tongue as the carriage came to a stop. Davis opened the door and let down the foot step. Rupert jumped down first and extended his hand to Diana. She took it and stepped carefully down onto the cobbled court in front of the Savoy's glittering façade. Her narrow heel caught in the space between two cobblestones and she was glad of Rupert's hand, which instantly tightened as she wobbled slightly.

"What ridiculous shoes," he commented in an unmistakably scolding tone.

"Thank you," she returned with a sardonic smile, removing her hand from his. Gathering up her skirt in one hand, she stepped delicately through the doors and into the brightly lit foyer. The maître d'hôtel appeared instantly, bowing deeply.

"Colonel Lacey, Madame Lacey. How delightful to see you again. It's been a long time."

"Indeed it has, Henri," Rupert responded easily. "My wife arrived in England only yesterday and her first wish was to sample the delights of the Savoy's cuisine again after such a long voyage."

"We are deeply honored, madame." He bowed once more to Diana. "I have your usual table ready." He clicked his fingers at a hovering page boy, who hurried to take Diana's shawl. "Please follow me."

Diana walked slightly ahead of Rupert into the familiar glitter and gold of the dining room. A discreet buzz of conversation filled the air as they threaded between the tall pillars, beneath the brilliantly faceted crystal chandeliers. She wondered which white-draped table was considered to be theirs because she couldn't remember dining here *a deux* with Rupert, although they had frequently been part of large groups of debutantes and their escorts during her come-out season.

The maître d'hôtel stopped at a table in the middle of the dining room. "I trust this is to your liking, sir . . . madame?"

Diana was about to say she would like a much more secluded spot behind a pillar, and in a corner if possible, but Rupert immediately said it would suit them very well and pulled out a cushioned, gilded chair for her. "My dear." He smiled and pushed in her chair, before taking his own seat across from her.

"A bottle of the 'widow' as usual, sir?"

"Thank you, Henri."

There was more finger snapping, sotto voce orders issued to an attentive waiter and a bottle of Veuve Clicquot appeared in an ice bucket. The cork popped softly, and Diana watched the creamy bubbles fill her champagne glass, the bottle expertly raised just at the moment the froth was about to spill over the crystal rim.

Embossed menus were placed in front of them, but Rupert waved them away. "We'll have the oysters and Dover sole . . . on the bone, my dear, or off?"

"Thank you for asking," Diana muttered. She smiled at Henri. "Do the work for me, please. And I'd like just brown butter, no capers."

"Of course, madame." Henri moved away in stately fashion, the buzz of voices continuing around them.

Diana stripped off her gloves and placed them on her lap. "You seemed very sure of what I'd like to eat," she said, breaking a warm bread roll.

"It was always your favorite meal," Rupert replied. "Was I wrong?"

"Actually I had thought to eat snails and roast duck," she said.

"Fibber," he accused, laughter enlivening his green eyes. "You hate snails."

And somehow, Diana could not help an answering glint of amusement in her own eyes. "I do like duck, though."

"Do you want to change the order?"

She shook her head. "No, I'm content with the sole. Pass the butter, please."

He gave an exaggerated sigh of relief and passed

the glass dish of butter across the table. "Do you see any familiar faces?"

Diana let her gaze roam around the dining room. "A few." She raised a hand slightly to acknowledge a smiling wave from a woman at a table across the room. "Letty Merriman is over there with a man I don't recognize, and Peter Mayhew is dining with Beth Carson. How long have they been interested in each other?" This kind of chatter was so familiar, so easy, that for a moment she forgot why they were here and began to enjoy herself as the champagne slid down and her eyes darted around the room.

Chapter Eight

Rupert watched her over the rim of his glass. His instinct had been right. If Diana could be diverted from her grief for her brother, however temporarily, and from the painful, angry memories of their own parting, she could relax, could once again be her old self. The strain had left her eyes, her mouth was soft and full once more, a natural smile on her lips. Her complexion once again glowed as he remembered it, the pallor and drawn look of the last two days vanished.

"What are you looking at?" she asked, suddenly aware of his intent gaze.

"Just you," he said simply.

Diana couldn't think of a response and was glad of the diversion when a waiter set in front of her a silver platter where craggy gray shells rested on a bed of ice.

Rupert leaned back a little as the waiter set down his own platter. He raised his glass in a silent toast. Diana followed suit before selecting an oyster.

She tipped the opalescent morsel straight into her mouth, savoring the briny juice. "I'd almost forgotten how good they are," she said, selecting another one. "You miss them in South Africa."

Nothing more was said until they had finished, then Diana dabbed at her mouth with her napkin and said, "There's something we have not discussed about this deplorable arrangement you're insisting on."

He raised an eyebrow. "Oh, and what is that?"

"Well, it seems to me that, while this pretend marriage suits you and does not in any way prevent you from doing whatever else you wish to do, it raises the question of what I am supposed to do if I wish to take a lover. I don't intend to live the rest of my life under a vow of chastity. And even more to the point, what happens when I meet someone I want to marry? I'm going to want children . . . did that ever occur to you?" Her voice was low but nonetheless vehement.

So much for social diversion, Rupert reflected ruefully. He hadn't expected this, or at least not this evening. It was obviously going to come up at some time, but he'd hoped by the time it did, they would have reached a point . . . a point at which the subject was moot. He was beginning now to wonder if that was a pipe dream.

He took a sip of champagne. "I had thought of it, of course. And I assumed, as far as lovers were concerned, we would give each other carte blanche. Obviously, if you're thinking of marriage, I will make myself scarce."

"How?" she demanded. "You can't simply undo a

marriage, even if it only exists as a charade. Not without exposing the charade, and I can't imagine how that would appear to any possible husband."

"I suggest you leave that to me," he stated.

Diana swallowed the stream of invective hovering on the tip of her tongue at such a condescending statement and folded her lips tightly as her Dover sole was set in front of her. She drank her champagne in fuming silence until they were once more alone. "Going through the divorce court seems like an unnecessary rigamarole to bring a sham marriage to an end."

"As I said, if that situation arises, you can leave it to me to sort out."

"That's so patronizing," she exclaimed, her voice low but fierce. "You put me in this impossible situation, one that's going to ruin my life, and then pat me on the head and tell me not to worry about anything."

"I didn't mean to be patronizing, but, sweet heaven, Diana, you do create minefields where they don't exist."

Her eyes narrowed. "Oh, and who says they don't exist? It didn't occur to you, I suppose, that I might have met someone on the ship?" She hadn't, as it happened, but she relished the startled look of chagrin in his eyes.

"Did you?" he asked after a moment's silence.

She wanted to lie, but it wasn't an untruth she could maintain. He would be bound to notice the conspicuous absence of such a suitor. "No, as it happens. But there are plenty of eligible young men in town at the moment. One might take my fancy at any moment."

"In that case, my dear, I suggest we suspend this discussion until it happens."

He turned his attention to his fish with a smile that infuriated Diana as much as his dismissive tone. She set down her knife and fork, laid her napkin on the table, and pushed back her chair. She spoke in an icy undertone. "I can't sit through this a moment longer, so I am leaving now. I will not draw attention to myself as I leave. If anyone notices me leaving, they'll assume I'm visiting the cloakroom." She stood up and left the table before Rupert could react. She walked through the busy dining room and out into the relative peace of the foyer.

"May I call your carriage, madame?" the doorman inquired as she paused to gather her thoughts.

"Call me a hackney, please." She walked out onto the cobbled court as the doorman blew his whistle to summon a hackney from the line waiting along the Strand.

"For God's sake, Diana, what d'you think you're doing?" Rupert stepped out behind her. "Come back inside."

"If you're worried about appearances, tell Henri that I'm suddenly unwell," she said without turning to look at him. "I'm taking a hackney home."

"No, you are not," he stated flatly, putting a hand on her arm.

Diana shook him off and stepped away hastily as a hackney bowled up to the hotel's front entrance. She took a hurried step onto the cobbles, and her heel caught again. This time her ankle twisted, and the thin delicate heel snapped. She stifled a cry of pain and exasperation, clutching a pillar for balance as she lifted her foot clear of the ground. She swore under her breath at the broken heel dangling from her shoe, for the moment forgetting the pain in her ankle.

The doorman, who had opened the door of the hackney, quickly came over to her. "Are you hurt, madame? Let me help you to the carriage."

"There's no need for that. And no need for the hackney. My brougham and driver are waiting in the side court. Send someone to fetch them, would you?" Rupert spoke with brisk authority, and the doorman hurried away immediately, leaving Diana clinging to the pillar, unable to countermand Rupert's orders or walk away herself.

"I am quite capable of getting home on my own," she hissed through clenched teeth. "Go back and finish your dinner."

"Don't be absurd." He stood beside her until the brougham appeared.

Davis jumped down from the box seat and opened the door. "Are you hurt, ma'am?"

"No, I'm not hurt. My heel's broken." Diana pushed herself away from the pillar and half-hopped toward the carriage. She inhaled sharply as Rupert lifted her and deposited her inside the carriage in one fluid movement. "I can manage myself," she said, aware of the futility of her protests.

Rupert didn't dignify her statement with a response. He merely settled on the seat beside her and the carriage moved away, under the arch that opened onto the Strand, which at this time of night was teeming with pedestrians and carriages.

They sat in stony silence until Davis drew up before the doors of the house on Cavendish Square. Rupert jumped down and Diana hurriedly inched along the seat toward the carriage door, determined to get out to the ground before Rupert took matters into his own hands again. She should have known better, she thought grimly, as he leaned in and scooped her into his arms, holding her firmly against his chest.

"Dammit, Rupert. Put me down." She pushed against his chest, but his hold merely tightened. Davis unlocked the front door and opened it wide. Rupert strode into the house, and his batman returned to the box to drive the brougham back to the mews.

The hall was deserted. Of course, she had told Agnes not to wait up for her, Diana remembered. And Barlow, knowing Davis was driving them tonight, would have taken the opportunity for an evening off himself. They were probably both cozily ensconced with Mrs. Harris in the housekeeper's sitting room, and the dogs would be with them, which left her with no recourse against Rupert at his most commanding. "Put me down," she demanded again.

"No," he said calmly, heading up the stairs. "Not yet. I'm enjoying the feel of you." He shouldn't be teasing her, Rupert knew, not when she was so vulnerable, but somehow, he couldn't help himself, and besides, it was perfectly true.

"Oh, you're insufferable." It was more than she could bear, and she grabbed at his ear, twisting hard.

"Vixen," he said appreciatively, turning along the gallery to her bedroom. Shifting her in his arms, he turned the knob and pushed the door open. The velvet curtains were drawn and the gas lamps were lit but turned down to provide a soft light. The coverlet on the bed was folded over, and on the dresser stood a small Primus stove, a saucepan of milk, a cup, and a plate of sweet biscuits.

"Very inviting," he observed, carrying her over to the bed. "Would you please let go of my ear now?"

Diana's fingers opened, releasing his earlobe. She looked up at him, at his face bent so close to hers. An arrested expression crossed his countenance, and she was suddenly very still in his arms, a soft flush warming her complexion, her gaze holding his before fixing upon his lips hovering just above hers.

He leaned over and let her slip from his arms onto the bed. For a moment, there was a taut silence in the room, interrupted only by the faint hiss of the gas lamps on the mantel. Wordlessly, he came down on the bed beside her, resting on an elbow. His free hand stroked the contours of her face, and a flood of memory overwhelmed her. How many times had he done that in the past? Her body shifted slightly on the bed, her legs parting slightly, an infinitesimal movement she could not control, one that clearly issued an invitation. She kicked off her broken shoe and pushed the other one off with her free foot, aware only peripherally of the throb of her sore ankle.

Rupert's free hand drew up the folds of her ivory gown, revealing her long silk-stockinged legs. His hand moved down to cup one knee, then slid slowly up her thigh, his fingers reaching the bare skin above her stocking tops. Diana drew in a sharp breath, her lips parting at the light grazing of his fingers sliding round to her inner thigh.

Imperatively, she lifted her hands to grasp his face and brought his mouth down to meet hers. And when his lips locked with hers, a hot rush of lust stabbed her loins and she reached against him, her body taut and demanding. His lips were hard and yet soft, hot and yet cool, and behind her eyes rose the red mist of desire. There were no questions to be asked in this space and moment, no conflict demanding resolution, no feelings at all except this passionate wanting. And it was all so, so familiar.

Without moving his mouth from hers, Rupert reached up under her skirt and petticoat to loosen the ties of her drawers, pushing them off her as her own fingers scrabbled to help him. Her fingers moved to the buttons of his evening trousers, unfastening them deftly. His penis was hard, pressing upward against her belly, and her fingers eagerly reached inside his loosened trousers, reaching to encircle the hard, throbbing flesh. This was no leisurely lovemaking; it was an impatient demanding act of pure passion, one body seeking the other, groin to groin in an act that resembled a struggle rather than a loving conjunction. They fought together to reach their own personal height, a desperate competition to attain a climax before the intensity of lust peaked and fell. It was a purely selfish battle, and when Diana cried out as the moment came and she seemed to dissolve into a molten puddle, Rupert collapsed, his body heavy on hers, pinning her to the mattress.

Slowly, Diana came back to full awareness. She pushed feebly at Rupert, who instantly rolled off her onto the bed beside her, where he lay with his arm over his eyes, his rapid heartbeat visible beneath the starched folds of his white shirt.

"I'm sorry," he murmured. "I don't know how or why that happened."

"Neither do I," she responded, imagining what they must look like in this tangle of half-naked limbs and disordered clothing. An indecent spectacle, she decided, and tried to push her skirt down over her thighs, aware as she did so of the sticky residue on her skin. At least Rupert had had the wit to pull out of her before his climax. What a god-awful complication to an already desperate mess.

"I think you'd better go now," she said after another minute.

He swung himself off the bed, hastily fastening his trousers, tucking in his shirt. "I'm not accustomed to making love in my shoes," he observed somewhat distantly.

"Was that what that was?" Diana asked. She wanted to cry with confused disbelief. It couldn't possibly have happened. And yet it had. The stickiness of her thighs, the slight soreness between her legs, the lingering sensation of his fingers grazing her skin all told her so.

"Well, whatever it was, I suggest we both forget it ever happened," he responded evenly. "You should put a cold compress on that ankle before the swelling gets worse." He bent to pick up his cloak from the floor, where it had fallen, and walked to the door. "Good night, Diana." The door clicked shut behind him.

Chapter Nine

Slowly, Diana got herself off the bed, wincing as she tried to put weight on her hurt ankle. She hobbled into the bathroom and turned on the bathwater. Maybe cold water was best for her ankle, but the rest of her needed a long soak in hot water, where maybe she could dissolve the shameful memory of that unbridled lust. How could she have allowed that to happen? And, more than anything, how could she have enjoyed it so much. Instead of being disgusted by his intimacy, she had wanted more of it, had wanted to become one with him as so often in the past.

But she despised Rupert Lacey; he had deceived her and denied her even the satisfaction of an explanation or a hint of remorse. And now he seemed set on making her life a misery. And despite all that, she had allowed *that* to happen.

She sat on the bathroom stool to undress, stripping off her stockings, casting aside her undergarments, struggling out of her petticoat and the ivory gown, dropping them in a heap on the floor. She hopped to the bath and sat on the edge, swung one leg after the other over the side and slid gingerly down into the hot water. The water was heavenly, and she lay back, her head resting on the rim, her eyes closing as her tense muscles began to relax in the warmth. Her mind drifted as sleep beckoned.

With a sudden involuntary jerk of her head, she came back to the world around her. If she didn't do something quickly she was going to fall asleep in this warm cocoon. She reached for the soap, wanting now only to wash away any physical memory of those moments and get herself into bed and asleep. She would have a clearer head in the morning.

However, getting out of the bath with only one good foot proved to be a lot harder than getting in. She twisted her body so that she was kneeling and was planning the next maneuver when the door to her bedroom opened. She had left the bathroom door open and now stared in disbelief at Rupert, who crossed the bedroom and stood in the bathroom doorway. He had abandoned his evening coat, silk waistcoat and white tie, and wore only his trousers and the white evening shirt, the sleeves rolled up to his elbows, the collar button undone, revealing the strong sun-browned column of his neck.

"I've brought a cold compress and a bandage to strap your ankle," he said as calmly as if there was nothing in the least wrong with this picture. "It looks like you might need a hand getting out of there." Just as calmly, he took up a thick Turkish towel and shook it out, holding it up as he approached the bath.

"What do you think you're doing?" she managed, acutely aware of her nakedness. "Go *away*."

"I've just told you what I'm doing, and don't be coy. It isn't as if I haven't seen it all before." Bending, he caught her under the arms and lifted her up, wrapping the towel expertly around her. "There now. I'll leave you to dry. Where's your nightgown?"

"Agnes would have left it on the bed." There really was no point in further protestations, Diana decided with weary resignation. Not after what had happened. Clearly, he was not going to take any notice of her protests, and equally clearly, she could do nothing about it at the moment. She was exhausted, and her ankle was really beginning to hurt. She hopped to the stool and sat down to dry herself.

Rupert brought in her nightgown. "I'm going down to fetch brandy. It'll do you good in some hot milk."

She had managed to get herself to the bed and was trying to straighten the crumpled covers by the time he returned. He lit the Primus stove and set the pan of milk on it, then poured brandy into a cut-glass tumbler and took an appreciative sip as he watched the pan. Diana gave the bedcover a final pat and climbed between the sheets with a sigh of relief.

"Drink this and I'll wrap your ankle." Rupert handed her a cup of steaming milk fragrant with brandy and pulled the covers back to examine her ankle. "A compress will bring down the swelling." Diana made no protest as he pressed the cold compress against the swelling and wrapped her ankle tightly with a bandage. "There, you'll do." He straightened. "Good night, now. Sleep well."

"You too," Diana murmured, adding after a moment, "and thank you."

He turned with the little grin he so rarely showed. "My pleasure, dear girl. Very much my pleasure." He turned down the gas lamps, and once again the door clicked shut, leaving her drinking her fortified milk in a darkened room.

Diana awoke when Agnes drew back the curtains and sunlight filled the room. She struggled onto her elbows. "What time is it?"

"Gone ten o'clock," her maid said. "I didn't think I should leave you any longer." She set a small pile of visiting cards on the bed and plumped up the pillows behind Diana. "Lots of callers this morning, after your outing last evening." She poured tea and handed her the cup. "Colonel Lacey said you had hurt your ankle. Should I send for the doctor?"

"No, there's no need, Agnes. I'm sure it's fine this morning." Even as she said that, she could feel the throbbing, and the bandage seemed far too tight. She sipped her tea and began to riffle through the cards. Society's rules dictated she pay return calls, leaving her own card, after which it would be assumed she was back again in society and could receive invitations. So much for a leisurely reintroduction via tea at Fortnum's with Fenella and Petra, she reflected dourly. Rupert had precipitated it by last night's dinner, or rather aborted dinner, at the Savoy.

She closed her eyes for a minute. Her body was

remembering what had happened after, and she couldn't seem to control the sensuous memories, which brought a tingle to her skin and a liquid arousal between her thighs. Hastily, she pushed aside the covers. "I'm getting up, Agnes." Action, occupation of some kind, that was the answer. She would not dwell on what had happened. It was behind her, and that was that. It would never happen again.

"Lord, Miss Diana, look at your ankle," Agnes exclaimed as Diana swung her legs out of bed. "You can't be up and about with that. Let me look at it properly." She lifted Diana's legs back onto the bed. "Lean back now."

There was no gainsaying Agnes when she was intent on something, Diana knew from experience. Besides, she was quite anxious herself to see the damage. She watched as Agnes unwrapped the bandage to reveal her grossly swollen ankle.

"Well, you'll not be going anywhere on that," the maid said grimly. "Get back into bed properly, now."

"I don't need to be in bed, Agnes," Diana protested. "I can get dressed and sit in the parlor with my foot on a stool." She slid carefully out of bed and stood on one foot, holding on to the bedpost. "There, see. Now help me dress, please."

Agnes looked doubtful. "I think we'll send for the doctor anyway."

"We'll talk about that later, just help me dress now." She couldn't help the impatient edge to her voice. She needed to be doing something, not sitting around brooding.

Half an hour later, Diana left her bedroom clinging to Agnes's arm as she hopped along the gallery toward her parlor. Her fervent hope that Rupert would be out was dashed when he came out of the breakfast room and looked up at the gallery. "You shouldn't be using that foot," he stated, mounting the stairs two at a time.

"Exactly what I said," Agnes agreed with some satisfaction. "It needs the doctor, Colonel."

"I'm not using the foot," Diana pointed out. "I'm hopping, in case you hadn't noticed."

"You need a walking stick. I'll see what I can find later. In the meantime . . ." He picked her up again, ignoring her hiss of annoyance. "Where do you want to go?"

"My parlor. I have things to do."

"As long as none of them involves walking on that foot, I'll agree to it."

"It's not your business to agree or disagree."

He laughed. "Oh, I think you might find that it is, my dear."

"I'll fetch up your breakfast," Agnes said, realizing her supporting arm was no longer needed. "And I'll send Billy for Dr. Bolton. That's right, don't you think, Colonel?"

"Certainly, Agnes," he agreed.

Diana was struck dumb by the realization that Agnes and Rupert had suddenly established an alliance where she was concerned. And they were a formidable pair. For as long as she was unable to stand on her own two feet, she was at their mercy.

"Where do you want me to put you?" Rupert asked, carrying her into her parlor. "Sofa or chair?"

"Oh, just put me down," she demanded impatiently. "It doesn't matter where."

He raised a well-shaped eyebrow, but set her down on the sofa, putting a cushion under her injured foot. "I have to attend Lord Roberts, I'm afraid, but I'll be back as soon as I can."

"The longer you stay out of the house, the happier I'll be," Diana retorted.

He shook his head at her in mock reproof. "Don't be ungracious now." And he left, his soft chuckle hanging in the air.

He would try the patience of a saint, Diana thought, undecided as to whether angry and antagonistic Rupert was better than this apparently amiable, teasing, if annoyingly high-handed version. She'd invited the latter and had only herself to blame for that wretched, self-indulgent display last night. The reflection did not improve her frame of mind. But there was one piece of business that would: Kimberley Diamond.

She got awkwardly off the sofa and hopped to the escritoire. Dipping her pen in the inkwell, she began a note to Ben, the racehorse's groom and inseparable human companion, instructing him to prepare her for a move to the trainer's stables. She and her brother had had endless discussions about which trainer to choose, given the mare's temperament and her natural affinity for flat track. They had finally settled on one not far from Deerfield Court so they could be on the spot whenever they pleased. But if she wanted to keep Rupert in the dark about the filly's whereabouts, she would need to find somewhere else, farther away.

Diana gazed into the middle distance, tapping her teeth with the top of the pen. There was a

trainer in Yorkshire they had discussed, but then
had decided it was too far for the horse to travel and
would severely limit their own contact with her.
Also, it wouldn't suit Ben, who would have to be
with her, to be so far from the countryside he knew.

And the climate was harsher in the north. Rupert
had described the freezing winters he had endured
on his grandfather's estate before he had become
an honorary Sommerville. It had sounded wretchedly
depressing in the draughty mausoleum in the Yorkshire Dales with only a curmudgeonly old man for
company, but his parents had died in a typhoid epi-
demic when Rupert was four and he had passed
into the guardianship of his only other relative,
Sir Maurice Lacey. Sir Maurice had had no time for
the child, and as soon as he was old enough had
sent him away to school, where the little boy had
spent long, lonely summer holidays as well as the
school terms. Until he had become friends with
Jem Sommerville.

No, Diana decided, Yorkshire was not the place
for Kimberley Diamond. It would have to be the
trainer in Kent, where the climate was softer. She
wouldn't be able to keep the animal's whereabouts
a secret from Rupert, but it had been a silly idea
anyway. A childish need for vengeance that was
beneath her. She wouldn't consult him, however.
She returned to her letter to Ben.

She finished that letter and one to the trainer informing him that Kimberley Diamond would be
coming to him within the week. She would go to
Deerfield Court as soon as possible and accompany
Ben and Kimberley Diamond to the trainer's stables

to discuss a training plan. That would definitely take her mind off the muddle in Cavendish Square, and get her out of the house for a few days of respite from Rupert's presence. Maybe she could persuade Fenella and Petra to come with her.

That prospect cheered her up immensely, enough that she endured the doctor's examination of her ankle with courteous good humor even though she considered it a great waste of time because all he could prescribe was the cold compress and bandage binding Rupert had already taken in hand. He offered her laudanum for the pain, which she politely declined, and bade him good morning.

"Oh, and Agnes, would you give these letters to Barlow for the post?" she asked as the door closed on the doctor. She held out her morning's work.

"I'll see to it right away, Miss Diana. Now, you just follow Dr. Bolton's orders and keep that foot elevated. Perhaps you'd like some calf's-foot jelly?" Agnes was in full nursing mode now, and Diana repressed a shudder.

"I'm not an invalid, Agnes, and you know I loathe calf's-foot jelly. A glass of sherry would go down better."

Agnes tutted but went away on her errand.

Half an hour later, Diana was sipping her sherry and playing a game of solitaire to chase away boredom when she heard the front-door bell. A few minutes later, a knock at the door heralded the arrival of Petra, Fenella and two young men. Hera and Hercules uncurled themselves from the carpet and stood at attention, ears pricked, subjecting the new arrivals to an unnerving scrutiny.

"Darling, we had to come to cheer you up," Fenella declared, casually stroking the dogs' heads. "Don't look so suspicious, you know me." That seemed to satisfy the hounds, and they returned to the rug but kept their eyes fixed on the two men.

"We bumped into Rupert on Piccadilly as we were coming out of the lending library and he told us about your poor ankle," Fenella continued.

"And he said we should come to visit you to keep you off your feet, otherwise he was afraid you'd start running around out of sheer boredom," Petra put in. "And then we bumped into these two, and they insisted on coming with us. You remember David Hanson and Jack Marsden from before you sailed to South Africa?" She gestured to the two men who had accompanied them.

"Yes, of course." Diana smiled warmly. "We danced many a dance together during the season. How are you both?"

"All the better for seeing you, Diana," Jack said, his dark eyes drinking her in. She remembered vividly how attentive he had been during that season, how, if she hadn't been totally in love with Rupert, she might have returned his attention. He was a handsome man, tall, broad-shouldered, his fair hair glistening like gold dust, his blue eyes either intently serious or bright with laughter. And best of all, he was as good a dancer as he was a conversationalist. She had enjoyed his company.

David bent over her hand, brushing it with his lips. The ring on her finger seemed to her to blaze suddenly, screaming its significance. She took her hand back, curling her fingers into her palm and letting her hand drop to her lap.

"So, what happened exactly?" Petra asked, sitting down on the end of the sofa, carefully avoiding Diana's feet.

"Oh, I just tripped as we were leaving the Savoy after dinner," she said with a careless wave of her hand. "It was stupid, clumsy of me. And now the doctor says I'm to stay off my feet for at least three days."

"Oh, what a nuisance, we had all sorts of plans now that you've let everyone know you're in town."

"What kind of plans?" Diana asked.

"Well, riding in Richmond for one," Jack said. "You're such a splendid horsewoman, Diana, and the weather's perfect for a long canter under the trees." He drew up an armless chair to the sofa. "Of course," he added, "your husband would be more than welcome to join us."

Diana smiled blandly. "Rupert's rather busy these days at Horse Guards. He's an aide-de-camp to Lord Roberts, the commander in chief. Quite an honor," she added, hearing the touch of sarcasm in her tone and regretting it instantly.

"Well, he was mentioned in dispatches after Mafeking," David told her. "He was a hero, from all accounts."

Diana said nothing, and Jack quickly filled the silence. "We were so sorry to hear of your brother's death, Diana."

"Thank you," she said softly. "Colonel Lacey had all the luck that day." She had long wrestled with her emotions on that score. She knew Rupert couldn't be blamed for her brother's loss and his own survival during that grim battle, but it had been hard to reconcile her grief-born resentment with that rational knowledge. And now Rupert was enjoying everything that should have been Jem's.

"Petra, be a dear and ring for Barlow," she said, changing the subject. "We'll have a bottle of champagne. I could do with something bubbly to dull the ache in my ankle."

Petra obliged. Barlow received his instructions with a bow. "Perhaps a few sandwiches as well, ma'am? Smoked salmon, maybe a little crab on brown bread?"

"The hamper from Fortnum's arrived, then?" Diana said.

"Billy fetched it last night, ma'am. And the new cook, Mrs. Adderbury, has already ordered from the butcher and the fishmonger. She's baking bread at the moment."

"Wonderful." She turned to her guests as the butler left. "The house has been empty for eighteen months, so everything was at sixes and sevens, but things seem to be getting back to normal."

"It must be a relief after all that time at sea," Jack observed.

"It was a tedious voyage," Diana agreed with a dismissive gesture. She didn't want to talk about those long, lonely weeks when grief for her father and her brother had mixed with her own unhappiness at the collapse of the future that had once seemed so rosy. They had been weeks of emptiness when she had finally allowed her tears to flow, her anger and misery to hold sway. And now it was over.

Now it was time to start again. Her gaze flickered to Jack and then turned aside as he caught her glance.

How was she to have a future with Rupert such a dominating presence every day of her life, not to mention the charade they were playing for the rest of the world?

Chapter Ten

Rupert emerged onto Devonshire Street and hailed a passing hackney. "Cavendish Square," he instructed the driver as he opened the door. How would Diana react to his actions of the morning? He stroked the smooth oak of the walking stick he had bought her and wondered if she would use it. Probably not, he decided, or at least not when he was around to see her do so. She wouldn't want to give him that satisfaction.

Matters between them had taken an unexpected turn last night, but he knew Diana so well and was certain she would be regretting it now. He'd expected to be regretting it himself, but to his surprise, the memory recalled in the bright light of day brought only a smile of pleasure. But he knew Diana would hate the fact that by yielding to impulse she had lost control. Her natural response would be to do everything she could to preserve the conflict, to deny absolutely that things had changed in any way. He was still trespassing on her life as far as she was concerned, and she would fight him and her own feelings tooth and nail.

But he no longer felt inclined to join battle with her. Of course, he could agree to accept her offer to buy him out and leave her in possession of the field, but that would get him no closer to his goal . . . or to her brother's. Oh, he had wanted initially to cause her both inconvenience and annoyance before coming to terms, but now he wasn't so sure he still felt the need to punish her. He still needed her apology for the deep hurt she had caused him that afternoon on the banks of the Orange River, and when he thought of how she had thrown his ring back at him, breaking their engagement without the slightest attempt to heal the breach, he still felt a rush of anger. There had to be an accounting for that, but with a cooler head, he realized he would only get that when they had reached some kind of accord, where painful subjects could be addressed without instantly causing defensive anger.

Rupert decided he would continue to refuse to do battle, continue to treat her with a light, easygoing affection. It would infuriate her, of course, and he wasn't self-deceiving enough to deny the flicker of satisfaction that would give him, but eventually, he thought it would wear down her resistance. And then they could confront the past.

The hackney drew up outside the house on Cavendish Square, and Rupert jumped down, reaching up to pay the driver. He turned back to the door just as it opened and Fenella, Petra and two young men emerged.

"Oh, hello again, Rupert," Petra greeted him in

her usual carefree fashion. "Diana is still keeping her foot up, you'll be glad to know." She caught a frowning glance from Fenella and flushed a little as she remembered that Rupert and Diana were not on good terms. She shouldn't be treating him with all the warmth of old friendship in light of what he had done and was doing to Diana.

Rupert caught the glance too and understood its meaning. He made no reply, instead turning his gaze to the two young men with a nod of acknowledgment. "Hanson, Marsden. You've been to see my wife, I assume."

"It's good to have you both back in England, Colonel Lacey," Jack said. "The country is in your debt."

"Indeed, after the relief of Mafeking the whole country celebrated, church bells ringing from the most obscure country parish to St. Paul's here in London," David added. "We all wished we could have been there to send the Boers packing."

"There was nothing heroic about it," Rupert declared. "There rarely is when it comes to war. Good day to you both. Fenella, Petra." He mounted the steps to the front door, not regretting his cold put-down in the least. They were only a few years younger than he, but to him now, they seemed like ignorant, thoughtless schoolboys.

The door was opened by a liveried footman, who bowed deeply as he let the colonel in. Rupert regarded him inquiringly.

"Diccon, sir," the man introduced himself.

"Welcome, Diccon." Rupert gave him a pleasant smile and headed for the stairs. There was a very different atmosphere in the house, with signs of housekeeping activity everywhere. The doors to the drawing room stood open, and he caught a glimpse of several maids dusting and polishing, the furniture no longer covered in dust sheets. Obviously, Diana had wasted no time in getting the house up and running again.

He made his way to her parlor and knocked briskly. The dogs whined through the door. "Come in." Diana's voice sounded resigned.

With a slight smile, Rupert opened the door. Sun was pouring through the window, falling across the sofa where Diana half-sat, half-lay with her foot propped on a cushion, a book in her hand. A ray of light caught the paler golden streaks in her thick brown hair. He wanted to take out the pins and loosen the heavy chignon, running his fingers through the cascading locks, separating the various colors that gave the whole such a glorious hue.

He resisted the urge.

"You had visitors, I understand." He crossed the rose carpet to the sofa and stood looking down at her. "A pleasant visit, I trust."

"Pleasant enough, thank you," she responded, barely raising her eyes from the page.

Rupert hooked a small gilt chair with his foot, bringing it closer to the sofa. He sat down, twisting the oak walking stick between his hands. "You appear to have been busy hiring a household," he observed.

"Not me so much as Barlow and Mrs. Harris," she responded indifferently, her eyes still on her book.

Rupert leaned over and took the book from her

hands, setting it aside. "May I have your attention for a few minutes, please?"

Diana gave an exaggerated sigh. "Well?"

"I bought you this." He handed her the walking stick. "It should help you get around more easily inside."

She looked directly at him then, fingering the smooth wood. "Thank you, Rupert. That's very thoughtful." A little glimmer of a smile touched her lips. "I bet you thought I would refuse to use it."

"It had occurred to me," he returned with that disarming little grin.

"I'm not that ungracious . . . or childish," she protested. "Although you do bring out the worst in me."

"How unfortunate for us both," he responded and was gratified by her smothered chuckle. He leaned forward and lifted a straying strand of hair, tucking it behind her ear. "My fingers are itching to unpin your hair."

Diana had frozen at his touch, her breath catching in her throat. She could feel the warmth of his breath on her cheek. "Don't, Rupert." It was more of a plea than a demand.

He let his hand drop and sat back again. "I visited Lady Callahan while I was out. I explained about your injury and that you had sent me to pay a courtesy call in your stead—"

"You did what?" Diana interrupted, sitting up straight, gratitude and amity completely forgotten.

"Let me finish . . . you had said you wanted to forestall a visit from your aunt, and because you won't be in a position to pay any calls yourself for a few days, I did it for you. Should her ladyship insist on visiting you herself in the next few days, you'll be forewarned and able to prepare whatever you want to say."

"You had no right to do that," she said, shocked at this wholesale interference in her most personal family business.

"As your husband, it seemed only natural. Your aunt certainly didn't think my calling was at all out of place in the circumstances. She was very welcoming and offered me a very fine claret." He sounded almost smug.

"You are *not* my husband and have no business interfering with my family," she stated.

"In society's eyes I *am*, my dear, and as such consider it my place to accord your family every courtesy." He smiled what to Diana was a smile of complacent satisfaction.

She wanted to throw something at him, anything to wipe that smugness from his countenance. Their earlier moment of accord was as if it had never been.

"There's no need to look daggers at me, Diana. If you stop to think, you'll see I did you a favor. Your aunt accepts your marriage as a fact, even though she was somewhat surprised there'd been no formal announcement from South Africa. But when I mentioned your father's death, she immediately understood." He stood up. "I should warn you, she is much affected by Jem's death. I'm afraid there will be tears when she sees you." He returned the chair to its original position. "I'll leave you now. Has anyone walked the dogs since this morning?"

Mutely, Diana shook her head. She could think of nothing to say to him. He was cutting the ground from beneath her feet at every turn, and until she was mobile again, she could do nothing about it.

Rupert whistled to the dogs and left the parlor, not displeased with his day's work.

Diana impatiently swung her legs off the sofa and pushed herself upright. She grabbed the walking stick and took a tentative step. She found it was possible to walk without putting much weight on her bad foot, and the satisfaction of relatively restored mobility gave her some sense of restored control. Rupert was insufferable and had to be stopped, or at least neutralized. Trying to ignore him didn't work because he was clearly impervious to such attempts, and she couldn't ignore the elephant in the room . . . the treacherous responses of her own body.

Anger was no defense against the surging memories of the good times, when they couldn't get enough of each other, when she breathed him in with every breath, when her body yearned for him whenever he was not beside her. Until last night, she had thought she'd managed to overcome that mindless desire—anger and grief had been powerful defenses—but then . . . but then, last night had happened, and now she felt once again defenseless against the onslaught of an all-powerful passion that transcended her anger, even the hot-white anger that burned now at his unendurable interference, his complacent assumption of control.

She needed air. The windows were open, and Diana hopped and hobbled across the room to the deep window seat. Kneeling on it, she rested her crossed arms on the sill and drank in the warm fragrant air of late afternoon. The small walled garden was ablaze with the roses her mother had loved. She had designed the gardens both here and at Deerfield and had delighted in planning the landscape, planting her chosen flowers and shrubs. Tears pricked behind Diana's eyes as the image of her mother bending over a rosebush, pruning shears in hand as she carefully deadheaded the faded blooms, rose vividly in her mind's eye.

Diana sighed. Why couldn't she be more like her mother? Nothing had ever seemed to disturb Stella Sommerville. It was impossible to imagine her losing her temper. The strongest language her daughter had ever heard from her had been the occasional, "Oh drat," when she'd put in the wrong embroidery stitch on her needlework or pricked her finger on a thorn.

Stella Sommerville would never have found herself in the kind of morass in which her daughter now floundered.

Chapter Eleven

"Of course we'll come with you," Petra declared two days later. "It'll be like old times. I love Deerfield."

"I do too," Fenella agreed. "It's been ages since we were there. Rupert's not coming, I assume."

"I'm certainly not inviting him," Diana responded, adding, "not that he needs an invitation anymore. However, I don't intend to tell him that I'm going. It's none of his business."

"Wouldn't it be easier if perhaps you didn't try to provoke him all the time?" Fenella asked somewhat tentatively. "I mean, I know he's done awful things and deceived you, but you are living under the same roof. You might be less aggravated by him if you treated him as a distant acquaintance rather than an enemy."

If only you knew, Diana thought. There was no conceivable way she could view Rupert in such a light, but she would cut out her tongue rather than tell her friends why. Her body's treachery was hard enough to acknowledge to herself.

She gave a light shrug. "You're right, of course, but every time I try to act like that, he does something to infuriate me again. He's so *managing*."

"Maybe that's got something to do with being a colonel," Petra suggested. "He's bound to be used to ordering people around in the army, and he does have a very important position as aide to Lord Roberts."

Diana couldn't help laughing. "Oh, that's so logical, Petra, but he's always had a tendency to take control, even when he was just a boy. And I'm ashamed to admit it does provoke me, and most of the time I think he does it deliberately just for that reason."

"You're as bad as each other," Fenella stated bluntly. "That's why we thought it was such a perfect match when you were engaged . . . oh, I'm sorry, dearest," she said hastily, seeing Diana's expression change. "I didn't mean to bring back bad memories. It just slipped out."

"That's all right," Diana said with a grimace. "It's good for my soul to be reminded of the humiliation now and again." She shook her head vigorously. "That's enough about Rupert for the time being. We'll take the train from Waterloo to Canterbury tomorrow. And we'll stay until we don't want to stay any longer."

"It'll be a relief to leave the city for a few days," Petra said, getting to her feet with a yawn. "It's so hot and stuffy, it makes me sleepy all the time."

"True enough." Fenella stood up. "We'll love you

and leave you for the moment, Diana. Are you sure your ankle will be strong enough to leave tomorrow?"

"It already is." Diana stood up, disdaining the walking stick to prove her point. "See, I can walk perfectly well." She took a few steps.

"You're still favoring that foot," Fenella pointed out.

"Only a little," she responded firmly. "We won't need to take any formal clothes for a few days in the country. We won't even dress for dinner."

"Sounds heavenly." Petra went to the door. "Hera and Hercules will be glad of the chance to run free." She pulled at the dogs' ears as they nudged her knees. "London parks are all very well for lapdogs, but not for proper dogs."

"Don't say that to the Monroe sisters," Fenella said with a laugh. "They worship their tiny little dogs. Last winter, I saw Leticia on Bond Street with hers in her muff."

"Each to his own, Fenella," Petra said. She kissed Diana's cheek. "Until tomorrow, then. We'll meet at the station under the clock."

Diana returned the salute and embraced Fenella. "If I remember aright, there's a train at eleven o'clock. I'll ask Barlow to send a footman to get us tickets this afternoon. We should be at Deerfield Court tomorrow by early afternoon." Rupert was generally at Horse Guards by midmorning. As long as he didn't change his routine tomorrow, she would leave the house and he'd be none the wiser. If he asked, and of course he would, Barlow would tell him she'd gone to Deerfield with her friends for a few days of refreshing country air. All perfectly innocuous and definitely not the kind of gathering where he would feel welcome. And while she was there, she and Ben would move Kimberley Diamond to the trainer's stables.

Using her stick, she escorted her friends down to the hall, the dogs bounding ahead, and waved good-bye from the door before turning disconsolately back into the house. Diccon closed the door behind her, and the house seemed to close in on her. After three days of house arrest, the sense of being trapped was becoming acute. The dogs whined in unison, looking up at her in mute appeal. She stopped at the stairs, making up her mind.

"Diccon, I'm going to walk with the dogs in the square garden for a while. I won't need a coat; it's warm enough."

"Shall I accompany you, ma'am?"

She shook her head. "No, I'm fine on my own, thank you." She added with a smile, "I have the dogs, after all, should I need protection." She walked out of the house onto the sun-drenched pavement, the well-trained dogs walking sedately to heel. Crossing the narrow road, she opened the gate set into the iron railings of the private garden. The gravel path circumnavigated the lawn and shrubs in the center, and Diana followed the path, using her stick at first and then tucking it under her arm to walk without it. The dogs raced ahead of her down the path but returned at her whistle, adapting to her pace, sniffing their way in leisurely fashion, crisscrossing the gravel as enticing scents beckoned.

Apart from a nursemaid sitting on a bench in the sun, gently rocking a perambulator, Diana saw no one else enjoying the sunny garden until she heard a step on the gravel behind her and a familiar voice spoke. "You're managing very well, but I wouldn't overdo it."

Rupert's voice brought her to a stop. She turned her head. "I don't intend to."

"Need some fresh air?" he inquired, sounding sympathetic, coming up to walk beside her. "Can't say I blame you."

He was using his charm again, and there was no defense against it except silence. So Diana merely showed him a tight smile and continued her circuit while Rupert remained companionably at her side. Once they were back at the gate again, Rupert forestalled her as she reached to open it. He leaned around her. "Allow me, ma'am."

"Thank you." She was forced to brush against him as she inched past him through the gate. Little electric currents sparked, lifting the fine hairs on her arms. The dogs hung back with obvious disappointment at the curtailment of their walk.

"I'll take them to Hyde Park," Rupert said. "They need a good run."

"So do I," she couldn't help saying wryly.

"Soon, my dear." Casually, he stroked the contour of her cheek with the back of a forefinger. "It's hard, I know."

If she gave him an inch, he'd take a yard. He took a simple, natural response to his comment as an invitation for an intimate touch. She ducked her head with a jerk and moved away from him, limping hurriedly across the street before anything else could happen to discompose her.

Rupert watched her go, waiting until she was admitted to the house, before whistling up the dogs and heading back into the garden. He took a narrow path that crossed the grass and let himself out of the garden through the gate on the far side.

Diana was reading a letter from the agent who supervised the Sommerville mines in Kimberley when Rupert returned with the dogs. A cursory knock was all the warning she had before he opened the door to her parlor. Hastily, she thrust the letter beneath the blotter and turned to greet him.

"Nice walk?" she inquired pleasantly, bending to caress the dogs, who were pressing their wet noses into her lap.

"The dogs enjoyed it," he responded with a slight frown. He hadn't missed her swift, secretive fumble as he'd entered the room, and he couldn't miss either the flicker of guilt in her purple eyes. Diana, incapable of deception, was a dreadful liar and a hopeless conspirator. *What was she up to?*

"You seem busy," he commented casually, perching on the arm of the sofa. "Anything I should know about?"

Two spots of pink glowed on her high cheekbones as she said, "Why would there be? My personal correspondence is nothing to do with you."

"No," he agreed, his frown deepening. "Your *personal* correspondence is certainly nothing to do with me."

The emphasis hung in the air for a minute, and Diana turned back to the escritoire, picking up her pen decisively, hoping he'd take the hint. Technically, she supposed she should share the agent's letter with the man who shared ownership of the mine holdings with her, but from her quick glance at the letter, it was clear the agent didn't yet know of Jem's transfer of part ownership to Colonel Lacey. At some point, Mr. Muldoon would inform him, but in the meantime, Diana saw no reason to take on that task herself. The letter was addressed to her and her alone; there was no need to give it to Rupert.

After a minute, Rupert stood up. "I'll leave you to it, then." He paused at the door, asking without much hope, "Will you join me for dinner?"

"I don't think so," she replied, keeping her eyes lowered to the blank sheet of paper in front of her. "I'm rather tired."

He shrugged and left the room, closing the door quietly behind him.

Diana slid the agent's letter out from under the blotter and began to read it.

Dear Miss Sommerville,

I trust your voyage was uneventful and you are once more safely in England. I am sending this to the London house, but I assume if you are in the country it will be sent on to you. I wish to reassure you that since the war's end, the workers returned without argument and the mines picked up work with production once more proceeding smoothly. The seams continue to yield a rich harvest and there is as yet no sign of that diminishing.

There is still much talk of the siege at Mafeking and the fierce battles it engendered. Mr. Jem

Sommerville's death continues to be deeply
mourned. He was much loved by our community
and the workers. I was surprised to hear that
Colonel Lacey was not present at the dawn battle
that killed your brother. Their friendship had
always struck me as close as that of brothers,
but I trust you are able to take some comfort from
the knowledge of the colonel's survival.

   I remain, as always, your faithful servant,
   Victor Marchant

Diana frowned down at the letter and read it
again. Rupert *had* been at that dreadful battle. In
the short note of condolence he had sent her with
the news of Jem's death, there was the clear implication that he had been at Jem's side, standing
shoulder to shoulder as always. And she had never
questioned his brief description of the events of that
dawn. They were no longer on speaking terms at
the time of the battle, and Diana understood he had
written to her out of duty and in memory of the past
they had all shared. She had accepted the letter in
that spirit and left it at that. It was too painful to
dwell on Jem's death, so she had merely skimmed
what detail Rupert gave her.

   She still had the letter, locked in the box where
she kept her most important documents. She got to
her feet and hurried from the room, not noticing
that she had forgotten the stick until she realized
she was limping. But limping quickly, she thought
with satisfaction as she reached her bedroom. The
room was empty, and she went directly to the armoire,

reaching up to the top shelf to take down the walnut box. She placed it on the bed and fetched the little silver key from a drawer in her bedside table.

The letter lay on the top of the stack of letters, documents and mementos. She lifted it out to reveal a pressed primrose beneath it. The memory of a bank smothered in yellow primroses was suddenly so vivid, she could smell the crushed grass beneath her, the light fragrance of the flowers, hear the soft gurgle of the stream below the bank. Her nipples suddenly hardened as if she could still feel the cool spring air on her bared breasts, still feel Rupert's hands between her thighs, a probing finger sliding into the opened entrance to her body, teasing, lingering, reaching, rubbing.

Dear God, just the memory could bring her to the brink of orgasm. She dropped the flower as if it were a burning brand and spun away from the box, thankful that no one else was in the room. After a few minutes, she took out the letter she had come for and unfolded it.

Rupert's familiar handwriting jumped out at her, every strong, definite, black-inked stroke redolent of his personality. She read it carefully. She had not been mistaken. There was one line, *we were standing at the redoubt when they came over the outer wall. In no time, they were upon us and we were engulfed.*

There was no mistaking the implication. He had been there, beside Jem, when her brother was killed. Somehow, he had survived and Jem had died.

So why had Victor said Rupert was not at the battle? Where had he heard that? Someone who had been there? Or perhaps it was just a miscommunication, the kind that happened when stories were passed from one person to another in a chain of gossip.

Yes, that had to be the answer.

Diana put the letter back in the box, locked it and returned it to the armoire, putting the matter behind her, turning her attention to preparations for the morning and the journey to Deerfield.

Chapter Twelve

Diana woke early the next morning filled with anticipation. She had always loved Deerfield, and the prospect of a few days' peace in the company of her friends and away from the tensions rife in Cavendish Square was very appealing. She slid out of bed and rang for Agnes, and was drawing back the curtains when her maid came in.

"You're up and about early, Miss Diana," Agnes commented, setting down the tea tray. "Shall I draw your bath?"

"Thank you." Diana took up the teapot and filled her cup. "It looks like another beautiful day."

"That it does. It'll be nice to have a few quiet days in the country," Agnes replied from the bathroom.

"I hope you won't mind traveling with the dogs," Diana said.

"Oh, they're always good as gold." Agnes came back into the bedroom. "But they look so fierce, I'll probably have a carriage to myself."

Diana wandered into the bathroom, shedding

her nightgown as she went. "I'll have breakfast in my parlor, Agnes, and would you let me know as soon as Colonel Lacey leaves the house?"

She toyed with breakfast, waiting on tenterhooks to hear that Rupert had left the house. He couldn't and wouldn't stop her going to Deerfield, but it had become vitally important that she make arrangements for Kimberley Diamond without his interference. She and Jem had planned the filly's future, and she was going to stick to that plan. Rupert must have nothing to do with it. Fulfilling Jem's wishes seemed to bring him back a little; she could hear his voice, see his intent expression as they mulled over various options. If truth be told, Jem's wishes had been paramount, and she had been content to have it so. Horseracing was an amusing hobby for her but had been a passionate obsession for her brother, and he had devoted all that passion to the filly. Now, she felt an obligation to fulfill his plan, that to veer from it one iota would be disloyal, an act of betrayal. If Jem's hopes for the filly came to fruition, Rupert would be welcome to half the proceeds as he was legally entitled to, and he should be satisfied with that.

Izzy the parlormaid came in to clear away the breakfast dishes. "Miss Agnes said to tell you, ma'am, that the colonel has left the house."

"Thank you, Izzy." Diana jumped up from the table and hurried out of the room, barely limping now.

Agnes was closing a portmanteau as Diana came into the bedroom. "Are you sure you don't want me to pack evening clothes, ma'am?"

"Quite sure. We're going to stay near the house and gardens, ride out every day and receive no visitors.

We shall dine in our dressing gowns if we choose."
Diana couldn't keep the delighted enthusiasm from
her voice as she began to feel truly lighthearted for
the first time in many months.

Agnes smiled and pulled the bell rope to summon
a footman to take the bags downstairs and then
followed him out of the room, Hera and Hercules
bounding ahead. Diana adjusted her straw boater in
the mirror, flicking the jaunty feather into position
with a finger. It was a light, summery hat that suited
her present mood. Satisfied, she went out onto the
gallery and was drawing on her gloves as she approached the head of the stairs, when she paused,
hearing voices from the hall below.

"Going to Deerfield?" Davis was saying, a surprised
inflection in his voice. "Rather sudden, isn't it?"

"It's Miss Diana's decision," Agnes responded.
"She's going with Miss Grantley and Miss Rutherford. It'll be quite like old times."

"The colonel didn't say anything about it."

"Well, I wouldn't know about that. What the colonel
does and doesn't know is hardly my business,"
Agnes replied somewhat sharply. "Ah, there you are,
Miss Diana." She turned away from the batman to
acknowledge Diana as she came down the stairs.
"The hackney is at the door."

"Good, then we'll be away," Diana declared.
"Good morning, Davis."

"Good morning, ma'am." Davis bowed. He said
nothing else, turning aside to disappear through
the green baize door to the kitchen regions.

Well, Davis would ensure Rupert wouldn't be in
the dark for very long, Diana thought with a flicker

of annoyance. But it couldn't be helped. She went out into the warm morning, where a hackney cab stood waiting. Sam had taken the brougham and her own riding horse to Deerfield the previous afternoon, and would be at Canterbury station to meet them off the train. She stepped up into the hackney, Agnes and the dogs following her, and the vehicle headed off around the square.

Fenella and Petra were waiting under the clock at Waterloo, the latter waving her hat vigorously as soon as she spied Diana, who hurried over to them, followed by Agnes and a porter. The porter piled Fenella and Petra's bags onto his trolley and they followed him onto the crowded platform where the train stood ready, steam hissing from its funnels. The porter found them an empty first-class carriage, placed their bags inside, then escorted Agnes and the dogs to a third-class carriage at the rear of the train.

"I packed sandwiches," Petra declared, indicating the small hamper on her lap. "Chicken and foie gras. Positively decadent. Oh, and a flask of sherry to wash them down."

"I had thought we'd have lunch in the dining car," Diana said, "but a picnic is a much better idea."

"They always have Brown Windsor soup in the dining car and I can't stand the stuff," Fenella declared. "Let's hope no one comes to join us." She stood up to draw the blinds on the glass doors leading into the corridor. "With luck, that'll put anyone off."

"I wonder how long the journey would take in one of those new motorcars," Petra said thoughtfully as the steam whistle blew and the train began to move. "Jack Marsden was telling me that they can go eight miles an hour. He wants to get one himself, but his father will have none of it."

"You can't stand in the way of progress," Fenella declared with a lofty air so unlike her that her companions laughed. She laughed with them. "I heard someone say that at the Criterion the other evening in just that voice."

"It's probably true, though," Fenella added, biting into a foie gras sandwich. "Who would have thought women would ride bicycles? I love mine. Of course, I can only ride it in the country, but it's wonderfully liberating, much faster than walking."

"Give me a horse any day." Diana took a sip from the flask before selecting a chicken sandwich from the hamper.

Rupert left Horse Guards at noon and strolled to the Army and Navy Club on Pall Mall.

"Lacey, come and join us," a voice called to him from a table set in the bow window.

Rupert raised a hand in acknowledgment and went over to the group of fellow officers lounging in club chairs at a round table. They had all served in the Boer War but now, unlike Rupert, were furloughed on half pay. He took a seat. "Sherry, please," he asked the hovering servant.

"You've been at Horse Guards," one of the group stated, taking a deep swallow of the claret in his glass. "How's our commander in chief these days?"

Rupert raised an eyebrow. "Lord Roberts is rather

occupied with ceremonial duties. I find myself with little to do much of the time." He nodded his thanks to the waiter who set down a sherry glass at his elbow. "So I'm afraid I have nothing newsworthy to report."

"This half pay is the very devil." A grizzled major flicked at the front page of the *Gazette*, which displayed an article on the army of furloughed soldiers kicking their heels now that the South African situation had been resolved. "How do they expect a man to live properly on such a paltry sum?"

"Well, that won't trouble *you*, Lacey," one of them in the red tunic and gold insignia of a lieutenant colonel of dragoons declared with a sardonic twist to his mouth.

Rupert looked at him askance. "What do you mean, Cartwright?" His voice was low, but there was no mistaking the edge it held.

Lieutenant Colonel Cartwright regarded him over a tankard of beer. "Well, not only are you still on full pay, but, as I understand it, on Sommerville's death you inherited his interests in the diamond mines and properties over there. Must amount to a pretty penny."

"So?" Rupert's voice was dangerously soft.

"So . . . nothing," the man said with a shrug. "It was just an observation."

"Is it true, Lacey?" one of the others asked, his eyes sharp with interest.

"As it happens," Rupert responded, draining his sherry, "and if you don't know already, you should also be aware that Sommerville's sister is now my wife." He stood up. "Good afternoon, gentlemen." He bestowed a cool smile on the group and walked off.

"There's a lot to be said for becoming close to the scion of a wealthy family," Cartwright commented. "Pity he couldn't manage to save Sommerville at Mafeking. I don't even remember seeing him there."

"Of course he was there," one of his fellows declared with a touch of indignation. "He carried Sommerville from the field. I saw him. He was covered in Jem's blood."

"Mmm," the lieutenant colonel said, burying his nose in his glass. "An affecting sight, I'm sure."

His companions looked uncomfortable, shifting in their seats, and then one by one took their leave. Cartwright signaled the waiter to fetch him another glass. He pulled the newspaper toward him and turned to the crossword on the back page.

Rupert entered the house on Cavendish Square and went into the library, where he rang for his batman. He was reading a pile of letters left for him on the oak desk when Davis came in. "Ah, Davis, bring me some bread and cheese, will you? And a glass of stout."

His expression, dark and forbidding, was one Davis knew well. Something or someone had seriously upset the colonel's equanimity. "Right away, sir."

"Oh, and do you know if Miss Sommerville is in the house?"

Davis paused, his hand on the doorknob. "I believe she's gone to Deerfield Court for a few days, sir."

Rupert's frown deepened. "Has she indeed. When did she leave?"

"Just after ten o'clock this morning, sir. Catching the train from Waterloo. I understand Miss Rutherford and Miss Grantley accompanied her." When the colonel said nothing further, he left the library for the kitchen.

Rupert stood tapping the letter he had been reading into the palm of his hand, staring into the middle distance. *What the devil was she up to?* She had to be up to something or she would have mentioned she was planning a visit to the country. It was not surprising she would want to go to Deerfield after being out of the country for so long, but why keep it a secret?

Was she just asserting her independence, her right to go wherever and do whatever she wished without informing him?

He wouldn't argue with that sentiment. She was not bound to him in any significant way. She was free to do as she pleased. *Unless . . . unless in this instance it* did *have something to do with him.*

He heard her voice in his head, declaring he was to have nothing to do with Kimberley Diamond. He had ignored the statement at the time because there were other battles to fight and the filly was safely tucked away at Deerfield. Time enough to enter the lists when decisions needed to be made. And now, he was convinced, Diana was making those decisions without consulting him.

The realization did nothing to lighten his black mood. He glanced at the clock. It was three o'clock, too late to get to Deerfield today. He'd take the first train in the morning, the milk train if necessary, and be there to surprise her for breakfast. His lips curved in a grim smile as he imagined Diana's reaction to her unexpected guest. It was almost enough to improve his mood. *Almost.*

When Davis returned with a tray, Rupert said, "Go to Waterloo, would you, Davis, and buy me a ticket on the first train to Canterbury tomorrow morning. Then pack a small bag for me . . . just enough for a couple of nights, but make sure I have riding clothes. I'm going into the country for a few days." He perched on a corner of the desk and broke a piece of bread, cutting a thick piece of Cheddar to go with it.

"Will you need me, Colonel?"

"No. I can look after myself for a few days," Rupert replied through a mouthful. If Diana wanted another fight, so be it.

The train steamed into the small station at Canterbury, and the three women descended to the platform, an elderly porter creaking toward them to take their bags. Agnes and the dogs came up behind the porter.

"Sam's outside with the brougham, Miss Sommerville," the ancient porter informed her, touching his cap. The Sommerville family were all well known in the town, Deerfield Court the most significant estate in the area. "Nice to have the family back again." He hoisted the bags onto a trolley and trundled it down the platform toward the gate leading into the street beyond.

Sam handed the ladies into the brougham, the dogs jumping in after them. Agnes settled herself on the box next to him and the horses set off eagerly along the familiar road. They halted of their own accord at the massive iron gates of Deerfield Court. A man emerged immediately from the gate-house, putting up a hand to shield his eyes from the sun as he hurried to open the gates.

"Eh, Sam, you was quick. Train on time, was it?"

Diana put her head out of the window. "Good afternoon, Ned. How's the family?"

"All right and tight, Miss Sommerville, thank you. It's a rare treat to have you back. And Miss Rutherford and Miss Grantley too. Mrs. Jones has been in a right tizzy since Sam told us last evening you was coming down for a few days." He turned and beckoned to a small boy who had appeared in the cottage doorway, staring curiously at the carriage. "Eh, Joe, run up to the 'ouse an' tell Mrs. Jones Miss Sommerville's just arrived." The child shot off up the drive at a run as his father pulled the gates wide to give the carriage entrance.

"There's no need for a fuss, Ned," Diana said, wondering how and when to make the staff at Deerfield aware of her pseudo-marriage. Maybe she could let matters ride for as long as Rupert didn't make an appearance. Time enough to deal with it when his presence made it necessary. "It's just a spur-of-the-moment visit. Mrs. Jones needn't go to any trouble."

"Ah, you know Mrs. Jones," Ned replied, shaking his head as he stood aside, waving the carriage on.

Diana pulled her head back into the carriage. "I

do know Mrs. Jones," she said ruefully. "And nothing will stop her making a fuss. Now I feel guilty for not giving her proper warning."

"Oh, she'll grumble, but she'll enjoy the challenge," Fenella responded. "She always loved it when you and Jem descended on the house with a host of starving friends after a day's hunting."

Rupert had almost always been one of the party too. With a little stab of pain, Diana remembered those good times when they would burst into the house, glowing from fresh air and exercise. Rupert and Jem would be arm in arm, and Rupert would be teasing her with the ease of long familiarity. In the very early years, his teasing had been of the elder-brotherly kind, but that had changed as their relationship had changed. He had still teased her with that old familiarity, but there was an underlying note of complicity, of something much deeper that they shared.

Abruptly, she stuck her head out of the window again. "Sam, stop here." When the carriage came to a halt, she flung open the door and jumped out. "Come on, let's walk the rest of the way. I love rounding that bend in the drive and seeing the house for the first time."

The three women descended to the gravel path. The dogs jumped down and raced ahead of them as they walked behind the carriage. As they approached the bend in the drive, Diana increased her pace. She turned the corner and then stood looking at the black-and-white-timbered Elizabethan manor house, with its four chimneys and its myriad diamond-paned windows glinting in the afternoon sunshine.

"It's such a pretty house," Fenella said, coming up beside her.

"Yes, and we always had such a good time here." Petra slipped her arm inside Diana's. "Playing sardines at Christmas and boating on the lake."

Diana remembered a particularly memorable game of sardines, when she and Rupert had hidden themselves in the attics so well that no one found them, and after a while had stopped looking for them altogether. Such memories were not useful, and she pushed them resolutely aside, setting off again up the drive to the front door.

Chapter Thirteen

"Lord love us, Miss Diana, here you are with hardly a word of warning," Mrs. Jones declared, as expected, coming into the stone-flagged hall, wiping her hands on her apron.

"Forgive me, Mrs. Jones, but I was so anxious to come home, I couldn't wait any longer. I've been in England less than a week." Diana came forward, hands outstretched, a cajoling smile on her lips. "It's outrageous of me, I know. But I promise we won't be any trouble. We could look after ourselves, couldn't we?" she appealed to her friends, who both nodded but looked a little doubtful.

"Nonsense," declared the housekeeper. "You'll do no such thing. The house has been ready for you, beds aired and made up, ever since I had your letter from Africa telling me you were sailing home. Dirk and the lad will take up your bags, and you three go along into the drawing room and Susie will bring you tea. Agnes, we'll have a nice cup in my sitting room. You'll be glad of one, I'll be bound."

"Well, that went better than I expected," Diana murmured as they obeyed orders and went into the drawing room. She went immediately to open the French doors that gave onto a wide terrace that ran the width of the back of the house. The dogs burst out ahead of her, racing around the grounds, tails flying. A balustrade separated the terrace from the sweep of lawn that led down to a lake, where a trio of swans paddled sedately. She stepped outside and inhaled the glorious scent of her mother's beloved roses and jasmine. "It's good to be home."

She turned back to the house. "As soon as we've had tea, I must go to the stables. I can't wait to see how Kimberley Diamond's doing . . . if she's recovered from the voyage."

"Did you decide on a trainer?" Petra made space on a table for the tea tray the maid was carrying.

"Jem wanted Cameron Thurgood, and he said he'll take her anytime. His stables are in Little-bourne, only ten miles away, so I thought I'd ask Ben, if he thinks she's sufficiently recovered, to take her over this afternoon, and I'll visit Mr. Thurgood myself tomorrow."

"This afternoon?" Fenella queried. "Why the hurry?"

"There's no point waiting around," Diana prevaricated, her gaze fixed on the spoon of strawberry jam she was spreading on a scone. "The longer the filly stays here eating her head off, the more unfit she'll get."

"Mmm," Fenella murmured. She had not missed Diana's quick flush, or the way her eyes refused to leave the scone or the jam-laden spoon in her hand.

"Does Rupert's inheritance from Jem include the horse?" she asked, biting into a buttered tea cake.

Diana sighed. Fenella always cut to the chase. "Financially, it does. He gets a half share of the purse if she places well."

Fenella only gave her friend a shrewd glance, but Petra said, "So you don't want him to have a say in her training. Is that why you're hurrying her away?"

"Yes," Diana responded flatly.

"Ah." Petra selected a cucumber sandwich. "Well, we'll come with you to the stables."

Diana nodded, her mouth full of scone.

Half an hour later, the three of them made their way to the stable yard at the side of the house. The dogs knew the way of old and seemed ecstatic at the familiar smells, racing from side to side in chase of elusive scent memories. Ben emerged from the stable block as the party came into the yard. He greeted Diana with a laconic wave and crossed the yard toward them.

"Glad you've come, Miss Sommerville."

"How's she doing, Ben?"

"All right, I'd say. She was off her feed for a couple of days when we got here, reckon the ship upset her, but she's calmer now and eating better." He turned back to the stable. "She's in the corner stall, more room there. I've been exercising her twice a day, but nothing to stretch her too much. She'll be ready to start training in a week or two, I reckon."

"I was thinking we might move her to Mr. Thurgood's stables this afternoon," Diana said casually.

"She can settle down there and be ready to start proper training in a week or so. What d'you think?"

Ben shrugged. "Up to you, Miss Sommerville. I reckon she's steady enough to make the move."

Diana followed him into the gloom of the stables, redolent with the smells of horseflesh, hay and leather. Dust motes danced in a beam of sun coming in from the half door to the yard. Hooves rustled in the straw of the stalls, long, sleek heads peered inquisitively over stable walls.

"She doesn't mind the company?" Diana inquired.

"No, long as they don't get too close to her. She gets skittish, then." Ben stopped at a stall in the far corner of the block. "Here she is." He reached a hand over the half wall and idly scratched the nose of the elegant animal within.

"Hello, beauty." Diana greeted the filly softly, making no attempt yet to touch her. "Isn't she gorgeous?" she asked her friends, who were standing discreetly behind her.

"Beautiful," agreed Petra. "Who's going to ride her?"

"We don't know yet. The trainer will probably make that decision himself once he's seen her move." Diana moved away from the stall, sensing that the highly strung animal had had enough of company, except for Ben's. "Will you take her over there now, Ben?"

"No time like the present," the groom said with his usual economy. "I'll tell Mr. Thurgood you'll be coming over yourself tomorrow, then?"

"Yes." She turned to Fenella and Petra. "We'll ride over in the morning, shall we? Merry could do with a good gallop, and there are four mounts for you two to choose from."

"Sounds lovely," Petra declared. "A country ride is just what I fancy."

They walked the length of the block and out into the late-afternoon sun, strolling back to the house to enter through a side door. "We're not going to dress for dinner, but I'd like to wash away the travel dirt," Diana said. "Shall we meet in the drawing room in an hour?"

They went upstairs and parted on the landing. Diana went into her own bedroom, with its mullioned window and low-beamed ceiling. Agnes had unpacked her portmanteau and set out her brushes, combs and toiletries in the small adjoining bathroom, which, while it had no hot running water, contained a claw-footed tub and a commode. An ewer of hot water steamed beside a bowl on the marble-topped washstand.

Diana stripped to her petticoat to sponge away the dirt of the train, reflecting as she did so that it really was time to modernize Deerfield Court. Once Kimberley Diamond was safely secured at Thurgood's stables, she would turn her attention to getting hot-water pipes installed. Was that something she would have to consult Rupert about? Surely he would have no interest in such mundane, quotidian issues. But maybe, just maybe, she could put him to good use, hand the project over to him and let him deal with it. Maybe, just maybe, there could be some benefit to her in this joint ownership. Lord knew the last thing she really wanted to do was become hip-deep in plumbing matters. And it would give

Rupert something to do that concerned the estate and keep him out of her hair.

The reflection brought a smile of satisfaction as she slipped her arms into a light muslin wrapper that was perfect for a quiet supper at home with her friends.

Rupert was the only passenger to step off the train at Canterbury station at nine o'clock the following morning. It was another glorious morning, and he savored the freshness of the country air after the heavy and decidedly unfragrant air of London. For a moment, he contemplated walking the five miles to Deerfield Court, but thought better of it. He wanted to catch Diana unawares, and even if she guessed he would follow her to the country, she certainly wouldn't be expecting him this early.

The stationmaster hailed him, emerging from his cottage, wiping his mouth on a checkered handkerchief as he swallowed the last morsel of a bacon sandwich. "You'll be wantin' the Red Lion's pony and trap, I reckon, sir. I'll send the lad to fetch it." He put two fingers to his mouth, and a shrill whistle startled a blackbird fluttering in the hedgerow alongside the platform. A small boy flew out of the cottage and took off along the road to town without waiting for instructions.

"Thank you." Rupert smiled a greeting.

The stationmaster came closer, peering myopically at the traveler. "Why, it's Colonel Lacey, isn't it? We wasn't expectin' you, sir." He touched his forelock.

"Not after what 'appened to Master Jem. Terrible thing, that."

"Yes, it was," Rupert agreed, but his tone invited no further comment. He had been a well-known guest at Deerfield for more than twelve years, but in the permanent absence of his hosts, it stood to reason that the locals would find his sudden reappearance rather odd. He debated telling the man that he was now married to Miss Sommerville, but decided that information should rightly come from Diana herself.

"I'll wait for the trap on the road," he said, picking up his valise. With a brief nod of farewell, he walked out of the station to stand on the roadside.

The inn's pony and trap appeared in minutes, driven by an ostler. The stationmaster's boy jumped down from the back of the trap and raced off without a glance in Rupert's direction. "Where to, sir?" the ostler asked as Rupert climbed onto the bench beside him.

"Deerfield Court, please." Again, his demeanor did not encourage conversation, and the man flicked the reins to start the pony.

Ned appeared to open the gates as soon as the ostler drew rein outside. He looked as surprised as the stationmaster at the trap's passenger. "Eh, Colonel Lacey . . . wasn't expectin' you."

"No, no reason why you should have been, Ned." Rupert gave him a cool nod.

"Miss Sommerville didn't say nothin' about you comin' down neither," Ned remarked, pulling the gates open.

Rupert made no reply to this, merely looked

ahead as they drove through the gates and up the drive, leaving Ned to shake his head at this deviation from the Sommervilles' customary way of doing things.

The house came into view around the curve of the driveway, and Rupert felt the rush of pleasure and anticipation he had always felt as a boy at the start of the summer holidays. It faded quickly, though, as present reality took over from nostalgia. He could expect a similar welcome from Mrs. Jones as he'd received from Ned and the stationmaster, unless Diana was ready and willing to smooth the path. He had hoped that when it was time to present the household at Deerfield with the change of circumstances Diana would be at his side, having accepted the fait accompli. Now, of course, he could expect no ready cooperation from her because her abrupt and secretive departure meant she had thrown down the glove again.

His lips thinned as the trap drew up at the front door. He jumped down with his valise and paid the ostler before lifting the brass door knocker and letting it fall with a resonant clang. Within minutes, the door opened, and an unfamiliar parlormaid stood looking up at him. "Yes, sir?"

"I'm here to see Miss Sommerville." He stepped past the girl into the stone-flagged hall, inhaling the familiar scent of the house, the faint residue of the winter's log fires blazing in the massive inglenook fireplace in the end wall, the lingering fragrance of beeswax and lavender oil.

"Miss Sommerville is not at 'ome, sir," the maid

said, looking at him with a somewhat fearful curiosity. "She went out straight after breakfast, sir."

"Susie, who is it?" Mrs. Jones came into the hall from the kitchen regions behind the oak staircase. "Why, it's Master Rupert . . . Colonel Lacey as I should say. Lord love us, sir. We weren't—"

"Expecting me," Rupert interrupted with a rueful smile. "No, I know you weren't. Forgive me, Mrs. Jones, but I came down to see Miss Sommerville on urgent business."

"Oh, she never said . . . not a word." The housekeeper shook her head. "But you've just missed her. She went out ridin' not fifteen minutes ago, with Miss Grantley and Miss Rutherford. Won't be back till teatime, I don't expect."

Rupert swore a silent oath. But there was little he could do. "Did she say where she was riding?" he asked without much hope.

"Aye, I believe the ladies were ridin' over to Mr. Thurgood's stables. Over Littlebourne way."

Of course she wouldn't waste any time. Rupert's expression gave nothing away. "Then I think I'll take a horse from the stables and ride after them," he said easily.

Mrs. Jones glanced pointedly at his valise on the floor at his feet. "Will you be stayin' in town, Colonel?"

He shook his head. "No, Mrs. Jones, I will be staying here. Diana will explain matters to you when she returns."

"Oh, aye?" The housekeeper frowned, then said, "Well, you'll be havin' your old room, then, I expect. Will you want Matthew to valet you?"

"No, that won't be necessary. I can look after myself." He picked up his bag. "I'll take this to my old room. Oh, and if you could find me some breakfast, I'd be most grateful. I took the milk train from London."

"There'll be porridge and kidneys in the breakfast room in twenty minutes," Mrs. Jones said with a decisive nod. "You always was partial to my deviled kidneys with a slice or two of bacon."

"Yes indeed. Thank you." Rupert gave her a smile that had her chuckling reminiscently. Master Rupert could charm the birds from the trees if he had a mind to.

Satisfied that he had handled the potential awkwardness of his arrival as smoothly as possible, Rupert took the stairs two at a time, turned into the west wing and made his way to his old room. He tossed his valise on the bed and his eyes went instantly to the door to the adjoining room, Jem's bedroom. He opened the door, pushing it wide. Nothing was changed. It was neat and tidy, the bed made up, just as it always had been. Just waiting for Jem to jump onto the window seat and fling open the dormer window, as he always did when he first got home.

Rupert stepped back into his own room and closed the door behind him, glad he had had the forethought to bring riding clothes. He changed swiftly into britches and a hacking jacket before heading back downstairs to his breakfast. The small breakfast room adjoined the old Elizabethan refectory, now rarely used, but Rupert remembered many big family occasions and Christmases, when the massive table had groaned beneath the traditional Boar's Head and the inglenook fireplace had been ablaze with logs the size of tree trunks.

The parlormaid set a bowl of porridge in front of him and put a chafing dish on the sideboard, together with a rack of toast, butter and marmalade and a pot of coffee. Rupert was ravenous, the smell of bacon irresistible.

"Anything else, sir?"

He shook his head. "No, thank you. This is perfect." He poured cream into his porridge and considered his options. Littlebourne was about ten miles away, an easy ride. Although he had never visited Thurgood's stables, he knew the trainer by reputation. The stables would be easy enough to find. And if Diana was there when he arrived, then . . . then he would give her the fight she wanted. Of course, she'd brought her own guard of honor with Fenella and Petra, but if she thought that would stop him, she was very much mistaken.

Chapter Fourteen

Diana dismounted in Cameron Thurgood's large and immaculate stable yard. There didn't seem to be so much as a wisp of straw out of place on the cobbles, the stable block was freshly painted, the half doors to the separate stalls open to the warm summer air.

"You could eat off these cobbles," Petra observed, dismounting beside her.

"More to the point, where are the horses?" Fenella stood looking around her at the peaceful yard, holding the reins of her own mount.

A man emerged from a building on the far side of the yard and strode toward them. Cameron Thurgood was as immaculate as his surroundings, in britches and gaiters, a well-fitting hacking jacket setting off his broad shoulders. "Ladies, welcome." He greeted them with a smile. "Miss Sommerville, I believe?" He held out his hand to Diana. "May I congratulate you on Kimberley Diamond? A magnificent filly. I watched her on the morning ride. Lovely stride, and Ben knows just how to handle her."

Diana beamed with pleasure. "My brother would be overjoyed to hear you say that. He was convinced she would do great things."

"I hope we can prove him right. Please, ladies, come into the office. You'll be glad of refreshment after your long ride. The lads will take your horses."

Two stable lads, who had appeared from another side building, hurried forward to take the reins of the three horses and lead them away behind the stable block.

"Where's Ben, Mr. Thurgood?" Diana inquired.

"Oh, Cameron please, no need to stand on ceremony. Ben's with Kimberley Diamond in the far paddock. We decided she would benefit from some freedom to do what she wants in the fresh air. Sea voyages take a lot out of a horse, so we'll let her feel her oats for a week or so." He led the way into a large office and gestured to the women to be seated.

After coffee and half an hour of horse-related small talk, Diana said quickly, "Perhaps we should discuss terms now, Cameron, and strategy for the filly's career. I don't want to take up too much of your time." Something she couldn't identify, a prickle of apprehension prompting a feeling of sudden urgency, was making her uneasy. She could think only that it was imperative to get the business arrangements settled before Rupert could interfere.

"Of course. Perhaps your friends would like a tour of the stables while we get down to business." Cameron rang a bell on his desk, and an elderly man appeared. "Ladies, this is Theo, our head groom.

He knows all there is to know about the stables and the horses we train. You'll find he can answer any questions you may have."

"I was wondering where all your horses were," Petra said cheerfully, jumping to her feet. "The stables seemed deserted. Come, Fenella, let's leave Diana to her discussion with Cameron."

The three of them left, Petra's stream of questions hanging in the air in her wake. Theo was as knowledgeable as promised and affably answered questions as he guided them through the stables and out into the paddocks.

Rupert rode into the yard just as Fenella and Petra returned in Theo's company. "Oh Lord," Fenella said as he drew rein in the middle of the yard.

"Now the fat's in the fire," murmured Petra.

Rupert swung down from his horse, handing the reins to a lad who had come running at his arrival. He greeted the women blandly. "Good morning, Fenella . . . Petra."

"This is a surprise, Rupert," Fenella responded. For all the blandness of his greeting, it was clear to both women that Rupert was not in a good mood to say the least.

"I doubt Diana will find it so. Where is she?" He flicked his riding crop against his boots as he looked around with interest at the orderly yard.

"With Mr. Thurgood, in the office," Petra told him, seeing little point in prevarication. "That building over there." She gestured. "We'll come with you."

"No, you won't," Rupert stated. "You'll forgive me, ladies." He strode off across the yard to the office building.

"Oh dear," Petra said. "Perhaps I shouldn't have told him."

"Of course you should. Diana knows what she's doing. Besides, how d'you think you'd keep it secret?"

Petra shrugged. "I couldn't, of course. We'd better stay out here."

"Definitely," Fenella agreed, seating herself on an upturned water butt. "Thank you for the tour, Theo. We'll just wait here."

"If you're sure . . ." The elderly groom gave them an imperturbable nod of farewell and went off into the stables.

"What I'd give to be a fly on the wall in that office." Petra perched on the water butt's twin.

Rupert knocked once briefly and then opened the office door, stripping off his gloves. "I'm sorry to be late, Diana. I'm glad you didn't wait for me." He gave her a brief, tight smile that contained only menace before turning to the trainer, hand outstretched. "Cameron Thurgood, I believe. Colonel Lacey. I share ownership of Kimberley Diamond with Miss Sommerville."

Cameron looked surprised and somewhat bewildered. "Indeed I hadn't realized . . . very pleased to meet you, sir. Please, take a seat. Can I offer you anything?"

"Not at the moment, thank you." Rupert set his gloves and crop on a table and sat down, crossing one leg negligently over the other. "Perhaps you could bring me up to date on what you've been discussing."

"Actually, Cameron and I have finished our discussion," Diana said swiftly. "We don't want to take up any more of his time, so I'll fill you in myself later."

"I would prefer to hear it from Mr. Thurgood," Rupert said without a flicker of an eyelid. "Perhaps you'd like to join your friends outside as you've already finished your discussion."

Diana shook her head and kept her seat. He was outplaying her, and she could do nothing to stop it, not without causing an embarrassing scene in front of the trainer. "We have agreed to the terms on which Cameron will take on the board and training of the filly," she told him. "I don't think we have to go over that again now."

Rupert looked over at her, his eyes flinty. "No, perhaps not," he agreed. "You may explain those to me later." He turned back to the trainer. "I presume you've watched the filly move?"

"Yes, this morning, Colonel." Cameron proceeded to repeat everything he had discussed with Diana, while she sat fuming in silence, and Rupert entered into a lengthy question-and-answer session with the trainer.

Despite her irritation, Diana couldn't help but acknowledge once more that Rupert was every bit as qualified as she was to talk racing strategy with Cameron. He made no attempt to suggest alternatives to the plan she had agreed on with the trainer: Jem's plan.

"I'd like to see the filly," Rupert said when the discussion had concluded, getting to his feet.

"Of course. I expect Ben's brought her back from the paddock by now. I'll take you to her stable," Cameron said easily. "You'll be wanting to see her yourself, Miss Sommerville."

"Yes," Diana agreed. She and Jem had bought the filly just before their father died, and she didn't think Rupert had ever seen her. But she couldn't be sure. Jem had maintained close contact with his friend after their engagement was broken, although he had always been considerately discreet about it.

It was an hour later when they were ready to leave the stables. Fenella and Petra held a subdued conversation on the ride back to Deerfield, while Diana and Rupert maintained a stony silence. As soon as they reached the house, Diana excused herself and went up to her bedroom, closing the door firmly, leaning against it with a sigh of frustration and futile anger. Was she going to have to submit meekly to this abominable situation? Rupert subverted everything she tried to do to assert herself, her own control of events. He made her feel like an obstinate child in the throes of a tantrum. And it wasn't fair.

She stepped away from the door, casting her gloves, crop and hat onto the bed with a venomous expletive. The door opened instantly. "I share your frustration," Rupert declared, stepping into the room. "Why would you try to outmaneuver me, Diana? I have every right to be a part of anything to do with the filly. You *have* to understand and accept that. I'm not going to go against you unless I think there is very good reason to do so, and so far I don't."

"The plans were Jem's, and I insist upon honoring them. They're nothing to do with you," she threw at him. "How dare you march into that office and take over the conversation with your masculine assumption of control—"

"My what?" he exclaimed, stepping up to her.

"Oh, you know very well," she said bitterly. "You instantly established a rapport with Cameron, as if you were chatting cozily in your club. I had just spent an hour going over every detail with him, and you waltzed in there and took over as if I wasn't there."

"Stop it, Diana." He put his hands on her shoulders and gave her a little shake. "I didn't do that. But even if I did, it was justified. You attempted to ride roughshod over any opinion I might have had, to deny me even a sight of the horse. You didn't seriously think you would get away with that, did you?"

"Oh, go away and leave me alone. I can't bear the sight of you." She tried to twitch away from him, but his hands tightened on her shoulders, and his face was suddenly very close to hers.

"Goddammit, Diana, you infuriate me—no, you *enrage* me, but I can't get free of you," he exclaimed. And then everything became confused. His mouth was hard, punishing on hers, and she bit his bottom lip, tasting blood, as she pressed against him, opening her mouth for his insistent tongue, scrabbling to get her fingers between the buttons of his shirt, to tangle in the dark hair of his chest, twisting in a frenzy of lust and anger. Nothing was clear, nothing made sense except this violent, urgent need. The buttons of her jacket flew apart as his own fingers roughly tugged at them, pushed inside her white shirt, feeling beneath her chemise for her breasts. He bore her backward to the bed, pushing her flat, pushing up her skirt, tugging down her drawers over her boots.

Then, suddenly, he stopped, leaning over her, his hands on either side of her face. "No, we're not doing this." She stared up at him in shock, her body thrumming. "Not like this," Rupert said. His voice was husky, his own desire a deep pulse. "I want to see you. I want to watch you climax. And I'm damn well not going to make love to you in my boots again." He straightened and swiftly yanked off her boots before kicking off his own. He stripped off his own clothes while she lay there watching him, her eyes drinking in every inch of him as her body throbbed with anticipation.

Naked, he bent over her again, pulled her upright and removed her jacket, shirt and chemise. Then he pushed her back on the bed, flipped her onto her belly and pulled off her drawers. "Kneel," he demanded, his voice low and filled with need.

Diana instantly drew up her knees, opening herself to him in the way that had pleasured them both so often in the past. He held her hips and drove deep into her, reveling in the warm wetness of her body's welcome. She pressed back against his hard belly as he moved inside her, but just as she sensed her body on the edge of falling into the abyss, he pulled out of her, flipping her onto her back, reconnecting in an instant, and this time he held her eyes with his as he moved slowly within her, watching for the moment when she was about to tumble from the peak. And at that moment he stopped moving, holding her there.

"Don't stop," she whispered, desperate now for completion.

He smiled. "As if I would. But I love to watch your face at this moment." Then he plunged hard and fast within her, and she heard herself cry out as her body convulsed around him, her legs twisting around his waist holding him hard against her.

Slowly, Diana came back to her senses as the world righted itself once more. Rupert lay inert and heavy on top of her, his face buried in the pillow beside her, his breathing swift, his heart beating fast against her breast. She let her hand fall onto his damp back, immobilized by the lassitude of fulfillment, for the moment incapable of coherent thought or speech.

After many minutes, Rupert rolled off her to fall onto the bed beside her. He lay on his back, his arm flung across his eyes as his breathing slowed. "Well," he murmured finally, "I don't know why you unman me so, my sweet, but I cannot help myself. I didn't come in here intending that to happen. I was ready for battle." He moved his hand from his eyes, dropping it heavily onto her belly. "What are we to do, Diana?"

"About what?" she asked lazily, a little smile quirking the corners of her mouth.

"Don't be obtuse," he said, turning on his side, propping himself on an elbow to look down at her. He ran a finger over her mouth, tracing its curve before bending to kiss the quirked corner, bringing a full smile to her lips.

"Well," she said, "how's this for a radical idea? Why don't we just stop fighting against the inevitable?"

"Ah, radical indeed." He hoisted himself up against the pillows, and she came up with him, leaning against him, her head in the hollow of his shoulder. His arm cradled her, his hand cupping her breast. "D'you think it'll work?"

Diana gave the question due consideration, her smile still on her lips. "Probably not all the time," she said. "But some of the time, I think. It's worth a try."

He laughed softly. "'Barkis is willing.'"

Diana chuckled with delight, lifting her hand to his face. "You remembered?"

"Always. How could I forget?" He turned his mouth to kiss her palm. "Reading *David Copperfield* with you that long-ago Christmas is one of my most-enduring memories."

Diana closed her eyes, remembering the long winter afternoons when they had read the book together, taking turns to read aloud. She had been fifteen, the year when she had become aware of Rupert as more than Jem's closest friend and her own quasi-brother. The recognition had made her awkward in his company, she remembered, and reading Dickens together had masked that awkwardness.

A sudden breeze blew in through the open window, cooling her bare skin and breaking the spell. She moved out of his arms, twisting around to sit up cross-legged on the bed facing him. "There's just one thing . . ." She plaited her fingers nervously. Everything depended on his answer, and she knew now how much she wanted that answer, whatever it was.

"Well?" Rupert sat up straight, his expression watchful as he wondered what was coming.

"Why did you walk away from me like that at the river, when I asked about the girl?"

His face closed in the way she dreaded, and her heart sank. She moved to get off the bed. "Never mind. Forget I asked." She stood up, her back to him. Her nakedness now bothered her, and she went to the armoire for a wrapper.

"Wait," Rupert said peremptorily. "Just wait a minute, Diana."

She stopped, keeping her back to him.

"Come back here." He patted the bed beside him.

Diana was unsure whether it was an invitation or a command, but she knew that if she refused there would never be another chance to recapture what they had once had. She sat on the edge of the bed, facing him in silence.

"Margery Ordway," he began. "She was the daughter of my grandfather's housekeeper. A buxom lass, and very much a country girl. A rather experienced country girl," he added, a sardonic edge to his voice. "And I was a very inexperienced sixteen-year-old. Inexperienced, but very anxious to learn. One school holiday she offered to teach me, and I accepted her offer. Boys of that age are generally in a hurry to lose their virginity. Innocence is not a quality to be proud of."

"Is that all?" Diana asked, more bewildered than ever. "Isn't she still your mistress? Aren't there children? That's what I heard."

"So you listened to idle gossip, believed every word of it and accused me of betraying you."

"No . . . no, you misunderstood. I wasn't accusing you of anything. I was expecting you to explain it to me."

"You didn't trust me. How can there be love, emotional commitment, without trust?"

"It wasn't gossip. Jem told me, and he never gossiped. He simply said you had strong feelings for this woman, that you felt some kind of obligation to her, that she had a child. He wasn't sure it was yours but said he knew you supported her as much as you were able. I just wanted to know the extent of your obligation."

"You didn't trust me," he repeated flatly. "Did you really think I would marry you without telling you of any other emotional or financial commitments I had . . . without mentioning a child, for God's sake? Why did you feel you had to ask me? I cannot abide mistrust, Diana."

Diana closed her eyes, pressing her finger and thumb against the bridge of her nose as she gathered her thoughts. Perhaps it had seemed as if she was accusing him of deceit. She certainly *had* wanted an explanation for what Jem had told her. Her brother had made light of it, as if it was perfectly normal, and she was not naïve enough to believe it wasn't. But she had been hurt that Rupert would keep such a vital part of his life secret. So, yes, she had mistrusted him. She certainly didn't want to believe he had had a mistress all the time he was declaring his love for her.

Well, in for a penny in for a pound. "Is she still your mistress?"

"No, Diana, she is not and has not been for many

years. But I am very fond of her, and I do give her money when I can. Life is hard for her and always has been. Her husband is a brutish wastrel, and she works her fingers to the bone trying to put food on the table for their children. Does that answer your questions? Are we done with this now?"

"Yes, we are, except that if you'd told me this at the beginning, we could have saved ourselves a lot of grief," she responded. "I refuse to take all the blame, Rupert. I can see that you might have thought I was accusing you of deceiving me, and maybe I *was* wondering whether you had or not, but I don't think that's totally unreasonable."

He was silent for a long moment before saying, "I don't know why I have such a visceral reaction to the idea of mistrust, but I do. My word is my bond, if you'll pardon the cliché. I need you to believe that if there is anything you need to know about me, I will tell you. Can you do that, Diana?"

"Yes," she said simply. "I can do that. But I need you to promise me that if something's upsetting you, you'll address it with me, not just walk away from it. Can you do that, Rupert?"

"Yes, Diana, I can promise that. Now come back to bed, it's getting chilly."

Diana slipped beneath the covers beside him, snuggling close, feeling his penis harden, nudging against her thigh. Chuckling, she reached down a hand to enclose it in her palm, stroking the damp tip as the shaft of flesh pulsed against her hand with a life of its own.

"By the way," Rupert said, his own hand sliding between her thighs, fingers probing delicately. "You didn't expect me to be a virgin when we first made love, did you?"

She gave a smothered choke of laughter. "Don't be ridiculous. Of course I didn't. I wasn't that naïve."

"That's a relief."

"You did expect me to be, though, didn't you?" She moved indolently beneath his reaching fingers.

"Yes. Double standard, I know. But I *had* known you since you were eight."

Diana twisted her body until she was kneeling astride him. She guided his penis into her, leaning back on her hands, moving her body in slow circles around his flesh buried inside her. Rupert smiled and watched her face as she pleasured them both. For the moment, it felt as if all was well with their world.

The challenge would be to maintain that state.

Chapter Fifteen

"We had better make an appearance for dinner," Diana said as the shadows lengthened with the sinking sun. She rolled onto her back with a lazy stretch. "Are you hungry?"

"Ravenous," Rupert declared. "I haven't eaten since breakfast, and I've been working very hard." He grinned and kissed her quickly before getting out of bed, reaching for his discarded clothing.

"So have I, and I haven't eaten since breakfast either." Diana propped herself on her elbows to watch him dress. "A bath would be nice," she added. "I was thinking the house really needs updating. It's time to have hot water put in, don't you think?"

"It would certainly be an improvement," he agreed. "Come on, get up." He reached down and hoisted her out of bed, then stepped back to look at her naked body with lascivious eyes. "Oh dear, I'd better go while I still can."

Diana smiled as the door closed on his hasty departure. She slipped on a dressing robe and rang for Agnes, who appeared in a few minutes with a jug of hot water. "I was wondering how long you'd be," she remarked laconically, taking the hot water into the bathroom. "Miss Grantley and Miss Rutherford are ready and waiting for their dinner. Sharp-set you must be, since I gather you didn't have luncheon."

"Yes, I am and no, I didn't," Diana corroborated, pouring steaming water into the basin. She soaked a washcloth and sponged her face before attending to the rest of her. Agnes was remaking the bed when she emerged from the bathroom. Diana made no reference to the untidy state of the sheets and covers, and Agnes kept a discreet silence.

"Is everything all right?" Fenella asked when Diana entered the drawing room. "You've been gone hours."

"We were worried," Petra added. "Rupert went after you and he looked ready to do murder."

"He was," Diana said. "But everything's fine now." She poured herself a glass of sherry from the decanter on the pier table, then offered it to her friends.

"Already have some," Fenella said. "Is Rupert joining us for dinner?"

"Certainly he is," Rupert stated, coming in from the terrace with the dogs. He poured himself a drink and smiled benignly at the three women. "Your health, ladies." He raised his glass in salute. "When were you thinking of returning to London?"

"In a couple of days," Fenella said, glancing interrogatively at Diana.

"We decided we would stay until we didn't want

to any longer," Petra added. "How long are you staying, Rupert?"

"I'll take the train in the morning. Lord Roberts will be champing at the bit."

"He does seem to take up a lot of your time," Diana observed. "But I suppose it's an honor to be an aide to the commander in chief."

"It doesn't always feel like that," Rupert remarked with a slight laugh. "Anyway, that's the way it is. Shall we go in to dinner?"

Three days later, the women returned to London, having satisfied their need for peace and quiet in country air.

"I do love Deerfield," Diana said, settling into the train carriage. "But after a while one needs more stimulation. I have to go shopping. All my clothes seem hopelessly out of fashion. Will you both come with me?"

"Yes, of course," Fenella said. "We'll go to Bond Street and Regent Street, and then we can lunch in Fortnum's. A real London day to make a change from the last few days."

"That's settled, then." Diana sat back, gazing idly out of the window at the countryside slipping past. How was it going to be with Rupert, now that they had reached some kind of agreement to cease hostilities? He was still living under the same roof, and she still couldn't rid herself of the feeling that he was there under false pretenses. And still she couldn't willingly accept the charade his presence forced her to play.

Unless it ceased to be a charade.

But even in the midst of their passionate love-making, nothing had been said about renewing their engagement. Not that there was any need to renew that; they could just as easily move straight to wedded bliss, a special license, a quick celebration with no guests and the charade would be reality and no one the wiser. But if Rupert didn't suggest it, Diana couldn't see how she could. She had broken off the original engagement and she didn't feel able to reinstate it as unilaterally. It would have to come from Rupert.

But did she actually want to marry Rupert?

That was not a question she either could or wanted to answer at this point, Diana decided. Leave well enough alone, and see what the future would bring.

"Penny for them?" Petra said, regarding her curiously. "You looked as if you're at war with something, judging by the way your mouth was twitching."

Diana shook her head. "I was having an argument with myself about something utterly trivial. As one does."

"As one does," Fenella agreed, shooting a warning glance at Petra, who frequently went where angels feared to. Not with any malice, always out of genuine concern. This time, however, the warning glance was sufficient. Petra ceased her questions and suggested they brave the Brown Windsor soup in the dining car.

They separated at the station. Diana, with Agnes and the dogs, took a hackney to Cavendish Square, while Fenella and Petra shared one to their own homes. Diana felt her heart beat a little faster as she went up the shallow steps to the front door, where Barlow stood waiting to greet her.

"How nice to have you back, Miss Diana. You had a pleasant visit, I trust." He took the valise from her, passing it back to Diccon.

"Yes, very peaceful, thank you, Barlow." Diana stepped into the hall, unpinning her neat felt hat. "Is Colonel Lacey in?"

"No, ma'am. He's at Horse Guards, as I understand it."

"Yes, of course. He would be at this time of day." She tried and failed to deny her disappointment. She was looking forward to seeing if anything had changed between them, now that they were back on disputed territory.

She was changing out of her traveling dress when Izzy knocked on the door. She came in with a note. "A messenger just brought this for you, ma'am. He's waiting for a reply."

"Thank you, Izzy." Diana recognized Rupert's bold black script immediately, and her heart quickened. She broke the seal, unfolding the single sheet.

I'm sorry I couldn't be there to greet you, dear girl, but I'm stuck in an interminable meeting at the c-in-c's bidding. Will you dine with me tonight at the Criterion? Unless, of course, you'd prefer a quiet dinner a deux at home?

It seemed Rupert was as anxious as she to see if their détente would continue under this disputed roof. Diana smiled to herself and went to her small writing desk. She nibbled the tip of her pen as she considered her reply. Which was Rupert hoping she would choose?

The answer was obvious, and she would have a surprise for him. She dipped the pen in the inkwell and wrote three words, blotted the page, folded it and stamped her seal on the fold. "Here you are, Izzy. Give that to the messenger, please."

Izzy went off quickly and Diana considered the evening. After a moment, she got up and left the bedroom, making her way down the back stairs to the kitchen. "Why, Miss Diana, fancy seeing you here," Mrs. Harris said in surprise. "Why didn't you ring for me?"

"Because I like the kitchen," Diana returned with a smile. "And I want to discuss a very specific menu with you and Cook." She took a seat at the long, flour-dusted kitchen table where the cook had been rolling out pastry.

"Careful you don't get flour on your dress now," Mrs. Harris warned, pulling out a chair and sitting down. "Mary, you'd best join us."

The cook, who, unlike the housekeeper, had not been part of the Sommerville household since Diana was a small child, was unaccustomed to these free and easy ways but perched on a chair, smoothing out the creases in her starched apron.

"The colonel and I will be dining in tonight," Diana told them. "I would like a very special dinner to be served in my parlor. I know I haven't given you much warning, Cook, but do you think you could do something special?" She gave the woman a cajoling smile, which brought a corresponding smile to Mrs. Adderbury's ruddy cheeks.

"What did you have in mind, ma'am?"

"The colonel is very partial to quails in aspic. Is it too late to make aspic?"

"Not if it's cooled on ice." The cook nodded. "Polly, girl, crush some eggshells to clear the broth," she instructed the kitchen maid. "There's some lovely marrow broth all ready in the pantry. Now, what else?"

"Roast beef and Yorkshire pudding," Diana stated with a laugh. "It's the colonel's favorite."

"Always has been," Mrs. Harris said, nodding. "And a duxelles of mushrooms."

"Exactly." Diana laughed. "With roast potatoes. Then Stilton mousse, followed by Ile Flottante. Can that be done, Mary?"

The cook nodded her head. "I'll send the boy to the butcher and the poulterer. Stilton, we have, eggs, cream, vanilla, everything necessary. Don't you worry, ma'am. What time do you want to dine?"

Diana glanced at the tall kitchen clock. It was already three o'clock. "Half past eight?"

"Oh, aye, that's doable, all right." Cook rose heavily to her feet. "I'd best get started on the Yorkshire. The batter needs to rest."

Diana left the kitchen and danced upstairs to her bedroom. "Agnes, I am dining in tonight with the colonel. And I will dress for dinner. But first, I need to talk to Barlow about wine, and then I have to go out on an errand." She hastened back downstairs to consult the butler on the state of the Cavendish Square cellars before leaving for Hoare's Bank.

"These are the final figures of the war's casualties, sir." Rupert placed the report on Lord Roberts's mahogany desk. "It seems we suffered rather more losses than the Boers." His voice was somber, the butcher's bill, as casualties reports were generally known in the army, was always the hardest reckoning.

"Mmm." His lordship examined the sheet. "Four thousand of the enemy to almost six of our own men. Nevertheless, Lacey, we won. That's really all that counts." He gave Rupert a satisfied smile. "The Orange Free State is now a crown colony and the damn Boers will have to like it or lump it."

Rupert made no response. General Kitchener and Lord Roberts were alike in their blithe disregard for the flesh and blood they expended with cavalier enthusiasm. His own ears still rang with the shrieks of the wounded and the battle cries of the enemy in full charge.

"Excuse the interruption, my lord, but there is a message for Colonel Lacey." An ensign stood in the open door, looking somewhat nervous. The commander in chief didn't like to be interrupted.

Rupert stepped forward immediately. "Thank you." He took the paper from the ensign and dismissed him with a gesture before saying, "A rather urgent message, my lord. Would you excuse me for a moment?" He slit the seal with a fingernail.

"Yes, yes, if you must," his lordship said testily. "What are we to do with these figures? Should we give them to the press? I don't want any shadow over our glorious victory."

Rupert glanced at the message. "*Dinner* a deux," and a smile touched his lips. He thrust the message into the pocket of his scarlet uniform jacket and restored his full attention to his master. "I don't think we can withhold the information, sir. If the press discovered we kept this from the public, they would have our guts for garters, if you'll pardon the expression."

Lord Roberts glared at the figures on the report in front of him, then pushed the paper in Rupert's direction. "See to it then, Colonel."

Rupert saluted, took the report and went into his own office. Half an hour later, he left Horse Guards and walked through St. James's Park on his way to Cavendish Square. Diana had answered his invitation exactly as he had hoped. An intimate dinner at home would end in only one way. And once this new phase of their relationship had become natural to both of them, perhaps past promises and commitments could be renewed.

"Good evening, Colonel," Barlow greeted him with a bow as he entered the house. "Miss Diana is expecting you in her parlor."

"Please tell her that I will join her in half an hour." Rupert strode upstairs to his bedchamber, summoning Davis. The house felt very different now from the way it had when he'd first taken up residence. Then, it had seemed more like a mausoleum than a family home, with an air of suspended animation, the furniture enshrouded in dust sheets. He hadn't known what to do to return it to the way he remembered it, but Diana had wasted no time in doing so. But then, it *was* her house. His own legal claim didn't really make it his, he realized. Well, maybe that would change now that they were at peace.

Rupert hoped he wasn't being overly optimistic as he changed out of his dragoon's uniform and into evening dress, but when he entered her parlor he saw he hadn't been. Diana was a vision in crimson velvet and diamonds. The gems flashed blue fire, encircling her throat and wrists, dropping in delicate pendants from her earlobes, nestled in the high-piled, rich coffee-colored hair. She was as regally attired as if she were attending one of the royal's drawing rooms.

She rose from the sofa as he came in, and her smile was pure mischief as she held out her arms to him. "What do you think?"

"Breathtaking," he said in awe. "You're magnificent, my sweet."

"I am, or the diamonds are?"

"Both. You complement each other." He gathered her into his embrace, inhaling the delicate flowery scent of her perfume, the richness of her hair, the essence of Diana.

"I've never worn them before," she said, fingering the choker at her throat. "I had to get them from the bank this afternoon."

"I think we can make good use of them later," he murmured, the lascivious glint back in his green eyes. "I have several ideas."

Diana touched her lips with her tongue, her skin

prickling at the promise in his voice, lust a sharp jolt in her belly. She moved away from him quickly as the door opened to admit Barlow and Diccon with the quail in aspic. She avoided Rupert's knowing smile and took her seat at the table, smoothing her napkin over her lap, hoping that movement would provide sufficient distraction from the surge of arousal.

Barlow poured wine. "A Puligny-Montrachet, sir."

Rupert took an appreciative sip, observing, "Almost as magnificent as the diamonds."

"I trust you'll approve the claret too," Diana said, finding her voice at last. If they could keep to small talk they might get through dinner before . . .

Later, much later, Rupert removed Diana's clothes, piece by piece, slowly, lingering over each inch of skin thus revealed. And when she stood naked in front of him, clad only in the diamonds' blue fire, he knelt before her, looking up her body, his hands tracing the contours, the angles, the curves and the straights of her. He slid a hand between her thighs, nudging them apart, and brought his mouth to her heated, pulsating core. His tongue dipped, probed, tasted, his hands clasping her hips, holding her steady as she writhed beneath his tongue in the glorious orgasmic explosion of pleasure.

She slipped to the floor, pulling him down with her, opening herself to him with urgent need. He entered her, joined with her in a climb to the heights and the long, slow tumble to oblivion. She held him against her body, her heels pressing into his buttocks as he buried his face in her hair, his body taut, his seed hot against her thighs. Her hair was tousled, diamonds winking in the unruly cascade. The diamonds were hard and bright against her white skin and her mouth was swollen, her blue-veined eyelids closed as the fever peaked and slowly faded.

Chapter Sixteen

The doorbell never seemed to stop ringing, Rupert thought at the fourth chime of the morning. Diana had a host of friends, and once she had reestablished herself in London society, most of them seemed to have taken up residence in Cavendish Square. Her assumed position as Mrs. Colonel Lacey appeared to make no difference at all to her popularity among the younger members of society, and there were times when he felt like an irrelevant outsider consigned to his work at Horse Guards and his books and papers in the library.

It hadn't always been so, of course. In the old days, before the war, he and his peers had been as much a part of the carefree social scene as Diana and her friends. But something had changed him. War had changed him. War and finding himself now a man of substance as well as an aide to the commander in chief at Horse Guards.

A babble of voices arose from the hall, accompanied by the excited barking of the dogs. He couldn't hear himself think and, abandoning his papers, he went to the door, opening it on a scene resembling bedlam. Diana was holding the hounds by their collars, trying to restrain them as they lunged for a small Pekingese, yapping from the safety of a young woman's arms. Several young men crowded around, offering helpful suggestions while the little dog's owner looked to be on the verge of hysteria.

"Dear God, what's going on?" he demanded. "Diana, let me take Hera. You can't hang on to both of them."

Diana relinquished Hera with relief and tightened her hold on Hercules, who began to bark at the yapping Pekingese, which promptly leaped from its owner's arm and scuttled across the hall to cower in a corner.

"I'll get it." Jack Marsden separated himself from the group and approached the terrified little creature. He scooped it up in one movement, holding it securely against his chest, stroking its head with one finger.

Rupert dragged Hera into the library, and Diana followed with Hercules, pushing the dog inside, stepping back so that Rupert could shut the door on them. There was a moment of relieved silence, broken only by the pathetic whimpering of the terrified Pekingese. Jack relinquished the animal to its owner and dusted off his hands.

"Sorry, Colonel, did we disturb you?" He gave Rupert a cheerful smile.

Diana said swiftly, "Thanks to your quick thinking, Jack, disaster was averted."

He turned his smile to Diana. "It was nothing, dear lady. You and the colonel already had your hands full."

She laughed, blowing him a nonchalant kiss before turning to the still-ashen dog's owner. "I am so sorry, Letty. I've never seen them behave like that."

"Probably because they've never been confronted with a dog the size of a rabbit before," Rupert put in dryly. "I suggest, when you're expecting visitors, Diana, you banish them to the kitchen, or bring them to me if I'm here."

"I don't always know when I'm expecting visitors," Diana said a shade tartly. Rupert was behaving like some kind of annoyed patriarch. She turned away from him, turning back to her visitors. "Jack, you deserve a reward, and the rest of you need something restorative. Come up to my parlor. We'll find a treat for Missie, Letty. She'll get over the shock soon enough. Rupert will look after the hounds." Linking her arm through Jack's, she turned back to the stairs, her visitors following her.

Rupert frowned at her dismissive tone. He felt relegated to some distinctly inferior role, and the cool assumption that he would take care of the dogs, while perfectly true, irritated him. He didn't like being taken for granted, and she also seemed inordinately flirtatious with Jack Marsden. A pleasant-enough fellow, certainly, but she really shouldn't go around blowing him careless kisses. He'd get the wrong idea.

Or was it the wrong idea?

Supremely irritated now, he returned to the

library, where the dogs, full of apologies, pressed against his legs, gazing up at him with soulful brown eyes. "That won't get you anywhere," he told them, returning to his papers on the desk.

It was over an hour later that he heard voices in the hall indicating that Diana's guests were taking their leave. He waited until he heard the front door close, then, growling a warning at the dogs, who were instantly on their feet, ears pricked, he stepped into the hall, closing the library door firmly behind him.

Diana and Jack were alone in the hall, deep in soft-voiced conversation. They stopped immediately he appeared, and he thought Diana looked a little flushed. Jack was holding her hand between both of his.

"Ah, you still here, Marsden?" He stated the obvious. "Sorry. I thought my wife was alone."

"I'm on my way, Colonel." Jack raised Diana's hand to his lips. "Thank you for that very fine claret, Diana. I'll hope to see you this evening, then."

"You may count on it," she returned, smiling. "Diccon will see you out."

The footman held the door and Jack took his leave with a deferential nodding bow to Colonel Lacey.

Diana turned back to the stairs.

"A moment of your time, Diana."

She stopped, her hand on the banister. "Yes?"

"I was wondering where you were going tonight? I had thought we might dine out."

"Oh, well, that would be nice, but I am promised

to the Grangers' soiree." She turned slowly back to him. "Why don't you come too? The invitation included you."

He shook his head. "No, I can't abide those occasions. I had hoped for some private time together, but—" He shrugged.

"You seem annoyed," Diana ventured. Despite their armistice, sometimes it seemed as if things were still not really running smoothly between them. She sensed disapproval in his manner, and he seemed to resent the constant stream of visitors to her parlor.

"No, it's just that when I'm working, I would appreciate being able to hear myself think."

Her eyes flashed purple fire. "If you cannot work in your part of the house, Rupert, I suggest you stay at Horse Guards, where I'm sure it's suitably quiet." She continued upstairs without a backward glance.

Rupert swore under his breath. He had hoped, once they were back from Deerfield, that things would be easier, but despite everything they had agreed, despite that wonderful night of the diamonds, Diana persisted in keeping her own life separate from his, her part of the house sacrosanct. It was as if they were two different people leading two different lives. At night they were lovers, their passion undiminished, but in the cold, clear light of day, Diana's resentment of his presence and the pretense she was obliged to maintain for public consumption was as fierce as ever. Until that changed, nothing else would.

Diana returned to her parlor and poured herself a glass of sherry. She took a thoughtful sip, wondering why she felt so out of sorts. And she guessed Rupert felt the same. Something wasn't working. They had agreed to try not to provoke each other, and she thought they were succeeding quite well, but they still led quite separate lives, and she was still adamant that they keep to their own parts of the house, except for the nights when he came to her bedroom. By insisting on maintaining this ridiculous pretense of a marriage, Rupert was imposing his will upon her, and all the lusting passion in the world couldn't change that. He was still being unreasonable in insisting on the absolute terms of Jem's will, and her own freedom of movement was seriously constrained as a result.

She would go and visit Petra, she decided. Her friend's company always cheered her, and they could go together to call on Fenella. She went to fetch her jacket. Rupert came out of the library as she came down the stairs.

"Going somewhere?" he asked.

"Just visiting. Why?" She heard the sharpness in the question and regretted it. They shared a roof; there was no reason why he shouldn't ask a civil question.

"Why so prickly, Diana?"

Instead of answering, she walked into the library, leaving the door ajar in silent invitation. He followed her in and shut the door. "Well?"

She sighed. "Nothing's changed, Rupert. A few passionate interludes don't alter the fundamental facts. You are forcing me into a position I cannot endure. I'm not free to be myself. You're always here, hovering like some hypercritical gremlin. You object to my friends, you complain about noise disturbing your work, but this is *my* house, not yours, whatever you may say."

Rupert frowned, massaging his temples. "There's no point going over old ground, Diana. You may resent me as much as you like, but I'm here to stay. And I really take issue with 'hypercritical gremlin.' Is that really how you see me?"

"You seem to me to be asserting your right to the house over mine. It's as if you think my needs and concerns are trivial, whereas yours are of earth-shattering importance."

His lips twisted. "Maybe I do think that. You want to play. I need to work."

She tried to fight down her anger. "I have to manage the estate, the administration of the mining in Kimberley, renovations to Deerfield, the house-hold here—"

"What do you mean, you're managing the admin-istration of the Kimberley mines?" he interrupted.

She cursed her unruly tongue. She hadn't told him of the agent's letter and progress report on the mining operations. "I didn't mean anything."

"Oh, don't lie to me, Diana. You're hopeless at it. What are you not telling me?"

"It was nothing, just a letter from Victor Marchant in South Africa to say that the workers were back, now the war is over, and the mines are producing normally. I answered the letter."

"Why didn't you inform me?"

"The agent was not aware of your part ownership and wrote only to me. As such, I answered his letter."

"You chose not to involve me."

"I imagine, once Mr. Muldoon makes the agent aware of your involvement, he will include you in his correspondence. It's nothing to do with me."

"May I see the letter?" His eyes were green ice, his voice uncompromising.

Diana bit her lip. "I'm sorry, I don't have it anymore. I threw it away after I'd answered it." It was the truth, and Rupert didn't question it.

He said, "In future, you will please share such correspondence with me. Is that understood?"

"In future, I trust you will be officially included and it won't be anything to do with me," she retorted. "Now, if you'll excuse me, I'll go about my business." She turned to the door, then paused. "Of course, you're more than welcome to take over the renovations at Deerfield, if you wish. I want to install hot running water."

"*You* want to?" he asked sardonically.

She turned back to him. "Yes, I do, and I assume that naturally you would too. We're not the ones who have to labor up and down stairs with kettles of hot water when someone wants a bath, and it seems to me that we should consider those who do. Don't you agree?" She raised her eyebrows in sarcastic inquiry. "I have a list of local plumbers, if you would like it."

"At your earliest convenience. Now, if you'll excuse me, I have work to do."

Diana spun on her heel and walked out of the library, closing the door with exaggerated care behind her. That whole encounter had been an unmitigated disaster. It seemed as if for every step they took toward amity, they took two steps back into hostility, and try as she might, she couldn't see any way to change that.

She left the house, strolling across the square garden on her way to Hanover Square, where Petra lived with her parents. The days of glorious sunshine had become a mere memory since they'd returned from Deerfield. The skies were now uniformly gray, and a chill wind had sprung up. She should have brought an umbrella and a thicker coat, Diana reflected, as she crossed Oxford Street, dodging between hackneys and vendors' carts.

Had she just missed the opportunity to bring up the strange lines in the agent's letter about Rupert not being with Jem at Mafeking? But Rupert had never implied he was anywhere else but at Jem's side during the attack, so if she questioned him, he would probably consider it yet another example of mistrust, another time she was questioning his word. And the last thing Diana wanted to do was dredge up that old quarrel. It was bad enough just trying to co-exist without adding fuel to the embers.

The butler admitted her to the Rutherfords' house on Hanover Square and took her jacket and gloves. "Miss Rutherford is in the small back sitting room, ma'am. Shall I announce you?" He handed her jacket and gloves to a footman.

"No, there's no need. I know the way, thank you." She ran lightly up the curved staircase.

"Diana, dearest, I'm so glad you're here. I've been pining for company all morning," Petra declared as her friend came into the small drawing room. "I'm full of cold, and Mama is fussing as usual. No, don't come any closer, you don't want to get it." She warded Diana off with upraised palms.

"You poor thing," Diana said sympathetically. "You do sound rather hoarse. Where did you catch it?"

"Mama will have it that it's all because I went rowing on the Serpentine with Charles Dexter the other day and it began to rain. It was hardly even a shower, but . . ." She shrugged. "I'll ring for coffee."

"It's miserable outside, so you're better off in here." Diana settled into the cushions of a velvet sofa. "Have you seen Fenella? I haven't for three days."

"Neither have I." Petra lowered her voice conspiratorially. "She's being rather mysterious. She said something about having lessons, but then she brushed it aside when I tried to find out what she meant."

"Curious. Lessons in what? I wonder."

"Shall we go visit her to ask her together?" Petra nodded her thanks to the parlormaid, who set down a tray of coffee.

"You can't go out with that cold," Diana reminded her, taking a cup from the maid. "We'll tackle her when you're better."

Petra sneezed violently, coffee slurping into her saucer. She fumbled for a handkerchief. "Where are the dogs? They're always with you."

"Oh, they're in disgrace." Diana described the bedlam in the hall, which sent Petra into peals of laughter. "Poor Letty was as terrified as Missie. Mind you, I don't really blame her. They can look dreadfully fierce when they want to." She sipped her coffee, wondering whether to confide in Petra about the agent's letter. It would be good to get another opinion.

She set down her coffee cup, thinking about how to begin when Fenella's deep, melodious voice interrupted her thoughts.

"Oh, you poor thing, Petra. I met your mother on the stairs and she told me you had a dreadful cold and advised me to stay away." Fenella came into the room as she spoke. "You do look peaky, darling. Do you mind if I just blow you a kiss?"

"Not in the least," Petra declared. "Sit down as far away from me as you can and I'll ring for another coffee cup."

"Oh, no coffee for me, thanks. I just had some." Fenella settled on the sofa beside Diana. "You won't be coming to the Grangers' soiree this evening, then, Petra?"

Petra sneezed into a delicate cambric handkerchief and said thickly, "I'd be persona non grata if I did."

"I think you should be in bed," Diana announced. "We're tiring you."

"No, no, you're not," her friend demurred, but without much conviction. She sneezed again.

Diana rose to her feet, Fenella following suit. "We'll love you and leave you, dearest, and come back tomorrow."

"I do feel rotten," Petra confessed. "Where are you going now?"

"There's a new milliner on Regent Street," Fenella told them. "I walked past this morning and there's a ravishing hat in the window. It's perfect for Diana's face, so I was hoping to persuade you both to come and look at it . . . but now . . ." She gestured sympathetically to Petra.

"There's no reason why you two shouldn't go," Petra said with a sniffle. "Show me the hat tomorrow, Diana."

"Well . . ." Diana hesitated. It seemed rather cavalier to leave the invalid alone while she and Fenella went off on a shopping frolic.

"I insist," Petra said, leaning against the cushions, closing her eyes.

Chapter Seventeen

Diana returned to Cavendish Square that afternoon feeling much more cheerful than when she'd left, swinging a hatbox by its silk ribbon. "Good afternoon, Barlow." She greeted the butler with a smile. "Is the colonel in?"

"Yes, the colonel is in." It was Rupert who answered her as he came down the staircase, the dogs at his heels.

To Diana's relief, he too looked to be in a better mood now. The dogs greeted her as if she had been gone for a year, pressing wet noses against her gored linen skirt. "You're slobbering all over me." She pushed them away fondly, and they sat gazing up at her in adoration.

"What have you got there?" Rupert inquired, indicating the hatbox.

"Oh, well, while you've been keeping your nose to the grindstone, I've been having a very frivolous time shopping," Diana said, immediately wishing she had not made this oblique reference to their earlier acrimony.

Rupert didn't rise to the bait, however, merely crossing the hall to open the library door, holding it for her.

Diana accepted the invitation, walking past him into the room, saying lightly, "I bought the most delicious hat, with a big floppy brim and silk roses in the band. It will be perfect for the October meeting at Newmarket. Cameron said he was thinking to give Kimberley Diamond a tryout then, just to see how she performs on the flat in an actual race. Depending, of course, on how she does in training."

"I'm not sure I'd agree with that." Rupert perched on the arm of the sofa, regarding her closely.

"Oh?" Diana looked askance. "Why not?"

"I think it would be prudent to keep her hidden and spring her on the racing world next summer. I don't think we should expose her too soon. Let her take the punters by surprise."

Diana considered this, idly swinging the hatbox. "You may have a point," she conceded after a moment. "But I'd like to discuss it with Cameron. He is the expert, after all."

"Certainly," he agreed.

Diana nodded. At least that had been a civil exchange of differing opinions. She turned back to the door.

"Are you dining in?"

Diana paused, one hand on the doorknob. She didn't turn to face him as she said carelessly, "No, a party of us are going to Le Dome for dinner before the Grangers' soiree. You did say you didn't wish to go to the soiree." She gave an expressive shrug but still didn't turn to look at him and so didn't see his frown and the way his face closed abruptly. When he said nothing, she continued on her way upstairs.

Rupert got to his feet, going over to the window. He stood there, hands clasped at his back as he stared out at the windswept garden. He didn't want to go to the Grangers' soiree—he'd lost all taste for such social diversions—and he realized he didn't want Diana to go either. But he had no justification for playing dog in the manger. They had agreed to act as if their marriage was one of convenience, which, of course, it was, he acknowledged caustically. *A sham of convenience.* But for the life of him, at present he couldn't see how to change that. He had woven them both into an impossible situation, and like a fool, he hadn't foreseen this consequence of his decision to manipulate Diana into accepting his reappearance in her life.

He was still in the library when the doorbell rang an hour later. He heard Barlow answer it, and the cheerful tones of Jack Marsden brought back his frown. The man seemed to be making Cavendish Square his home from home. He heard Diana call out as she came swiftly downstairs.

"Hello, Jack. You're very punctual."

"How could I be late with such a pot of gold at the end of my rainbow?" Jack responded. "You look wonderful, Diana."

Rupert, listening behind the library door, felt a renewed surge of irritation. Such facile flimflam from an overprivileged idler. He opened the door and stepped into the hall. "Marsden." He accorded the visitor an indifferent nod, forced to acknowledge as he did so that Jack Marsden was a very good-looking man. Evening dress suited his lean, athletic physique, and Diana, descending the staircase with a swift step, was inevitably aware of it.

She did look wonderful, though, in a low-cut gown of lavender taffeta with purple velvet banding at the neck, wrists and hem, a perfect complement to her eyes. Her pale complexion was delicately tinged with pink and she wore a sapphire choker encircling her long white throat. For a moment, he fought with himself, fought the primitive need to claim her in front of Marsden as his own. Instead, he had to watch as she gave Jack Marsden her hand, had to watch as he brushed his lips across her fingers, had to watch as she leaned in and lightly touched his cheek with her lips.

Her easy manner, her swift repartee, her ready laugh, so light and melodious, had always distinguished her. It made her seem flirtatious, but Rupert knew it was simply the way Diana was. She never paid attention to the formality of social convention, and it was one of the reasons he had first loved her.

She turned her radiant countenance toward him as she drew on her white silk gloves. "Are you sure you won't come to the Grangers', Rupert? We're going to dinner first, but we should be there soon after nine o'clock."

Was it a genuine invitation, or merely part of the pretense of an agreeable marriage?

It was impossible to tell. Rupert forced a smile to his lips. "Not tonight, my dear. I have work to do.

But you go and enjoy yourself. Look after my wife, Marsden."

He turned and went back into the library as Jack said to his back, "Of course I will, Colonel."

Rupert's smile had come nowhere near his eyes, Diana thought as she adjusted the fur wrap around her shoulders. But her movements were no business of his. She straightened her shoulders and accepted Jack's arm to the waiting hackney.

Strangely, though, she found that her natural ebullience had to be manufactured as the evening progressed. Jack was an agreeable escort, and the other members of their party at dinner were all people she had known since her debutante season. Fenella and her escort, Lord Singleton, were seated across from her, and she was aware of Fenella's occasionally puzzled glances in her direction. Her friend was as closely attuned to Diana's moods as she was to hers and clearly realized Diana was preoccupied, her conversation somewhat forced.

Fortunately, Jack didn't seem to be aware of anything out of the ordinary and seemed happy enough just to have Diana at his side. As they left the restaurant after dinner, he draped her fur stole over her shoulders solicitously, tucked her arm into his as they walked to the waiting carriage and handed her up with a distinctly proprietorial air.

And it didn't feel right. Diana struggled to keep a polite smile on her lips as she accepted these courtesies, but she didn't want them. At least not from Jack. Not that Rupert would bother particularly with such careful attentions. He had known her for too long and had never treated her like a porcelain doll that might break at the slightest knock. He respected her independence. He'd expect her to know when she was cold and to do something about it herself.

Of course, the other side of this coin was that he was just as likely to assume control of any situation he felt wasn't going the way he wanted it to. She couldn't imagine Jack presuming so far; he was too much the gentleman.

Chiding herself for being unfair, Diana made an effort to smile and thank Jack, resisting the urge to brush his protective arm aside, to ignore his helping hand.

Rupert ate a solitary dinner at Cavendish Square, wishing he'd gone to his club instead. At least he'd have friendly company there. But he guessed most of his army friends would be attending the Grangers' soiree. The Honorable Tim Granger had fought with them against the Boers but had given up his commission at the end of the war and settled into comfortable married life. Like most of the privileged young men who had bought commissions in the dragoons to fight in South Africa, he had family interests in the gold and diamond mines of the Transvaal. Once the threat to those financial interests was defeated, there was no need to remain in the army.

It was different for Rupert. He had joined the army with Jem, at that time with no interests himself in the disputed territory, but he had felt then that he had nothing better to do and, since the Sommervilles had been so good to him over the years, by fighting for their interests, he would be paying them back in some measure.

After Jem's death at Mafeking, Rupert had fought with a passionate fervor that had brought him to the attention of the high command. He had been twice mentioned in dispatches and, without any active decision on his own part, had found himself appointed to headquarters. After the debacle with Diana and then Jem's death, Rupert had no reason to leave the army, and because the army seemed to like him, he had let himself drift into the position in which he now was. At the beck and call of the commander in chief. And in an unholy tangle with Diana Sommerville. The image of Diana and Jack Marsden on the stairs rose vividly in his mind's eye.

He twisted his wineglass by the stem, frowning, then abruptly pushed back his chair from the table and stood up. He would go to the soiree, play cards with his friends and keep an eye on Diana. Anything was better than imagining what she was up to with Marsden.

Did he really think she was up to something with Marsden?

It wasn't a question Rupert wanted to answer. He went to change into evening dress.

Diana looked around the crowded salon. A small orchestra played on a raised dais at one end of the long room and a few couples were dancing. Voices rose and fell from groups of guests around the room. Beyond an archway in an adjoining salon, others were gathered at card tables. Servants moved among the guests with trays of glasses and silver platters of delicacies.

Jack weaved his way toward her with a plate. "I found caviar," he declared triumphantly. "I liberated it from a lieutenant colonel, who was not best pleased. But he'd put it down, so it was up for grabs. Have one." He held out the plate.

Diana laughed. "Well done, Jack." She took a square of dark bread liberally spread with the shiny black eggs of the sturgeon. She popped it whole into her mouth and savored the briny slipperiness. "Delicious."

"Excuse me, Marsden, but I believe that belongs to me." The loud voice came from a large man, whose ruddy cheeks and the slight paunch pushing against his white waistcoat indicated the beginnings of an overly indulgent lifestyle.

"Two more each and I'll happily give it back, Cartwright," Jack said with his disarming smile. "You did take your eyes off it, though." He held out the plate to Diana. "Take two, Diana."

She glanced at the newcomer, seeing his disgruntled expression. "I don't believe we've met," she said, holding out her hand. "Diana Sommervi . . . I beg your pardon." She corrected herself. "Diana Lacey."

Something appeared in his eyes, a quick, calculating look that disappeared so quickly, Diana thought she was mistaken. He bowed over her hand, but his disagreeable expression didn't change as he said, "Mrs. Lacey. Lieutenant Colonel David Cartwright, at your service. Lacey is twice blessed, it seems. A charming wife and her brother's inheritance. Some men have all the luck."

He laughed as if he'd made a joke, but Diana found nothing amusing in the comment. She merely looked at him, her eyebrows quirked in silent question.

"My congratulations, ma'am." He bowed again before relinquishing her hand.

He didn't sound particularly congratulatory, Diana thought, but perhaps the loss of his caviar had affected his manners. "Thank you," she said. "Jack, do give the colonel back his caviar and go and see if you can find a plate of our own."

Jack, always obliging, did as she asked. "Here you are, Cartwright. Although I do consider it fair spoils, I always obey a lady's request." He offered a mock bow and went off in search.

"Shall we sit down, Mrs. Lacey, and enjoy the rest of these?" Cartwright suggested, indicating a pair of empty chairs set apart in a niche.

Diana conceded with some reluctance. She didn't like the man. He made her uneasy. However, she sat down, her taffeta skirts settling around her. "I was well acquainted with your brother, ma'am," her companion commented as he sat beside her, setting the platter on a small gilt table between them. "Please accept my condolences."

"Thank you. You knew Jem well, then?" Despite her unease, Diana couldn't resist the opportunity to discuss her brother.

"We were in the same regiment, but also in the same corps. Together with our host . . . and Colonel Lacey," he added after a moment's hesitation, so brief it was hardly noticeable. But Diana noticed it.

"Indeed," she said. "Were you at Mafeking?"

"Yes, I was." His expression darkened. "I was close to your brother when he was killed in the first charge."

Diana's heart seemed to pause its regular rhythm. "You saw him die?" she asked with difficulty. "My husband was beside him, but I have never asked him exactly what happened." She closed her eyes for a second, remembering Rupert's exact words in the letter he had sent her, telling her of her brother's death. "He explained that Jem died of a bayonet thrust, but in the darkness and chaos of the attack, he couldn't be certain of the details . . . of how it happened."

"Really?" Cartwright's eyebrows lifted a fraction. "I wasn't aware your husband was in the line of defense at the time of the attack. But, of course, I could have missed seeing him." A thin smile touched his mouth and his tone held a note of incredulity. "It was certainly chaotic, but the sun had just risen, so there was light. I witnessed every moment of the charge. And I saw clearly the bayonet thrust that killed your brother."

Diana was aware of a coldness on the back of her neck, a slight shiver down her spine. Why were people telling her that Rupert wasn't there beside Jem, supporting him against the enemy's charge? Rupert had said unequivocally that he *had* been there. Why would he lie?

But she had promised to trust him. To accept his word on the understanding that he would tell her anything that concerned her.

"I expect Colonel Lacey's attention was diverted in the attack," she said with a vaguely dismissive gesture.

"It must have been almost impossible to keep track of events in such a violent furor." She looked around, desperate for a diversion, and saw with relief Jack weaving his way through the throng toward them, holding a platter aloft. "Jack, did you have any luck?" she greeted him with a welcoming smile, relief clear in her eyes and voice.

"I'll take my leave." Lieutenant Colonel Cartwright got to his feet, bowed to Diana with a cold smile. "A pleasure, Mrs. Lacey. If you'll excuse me . . . Marsden." He accorded Jack a cool nod and disappeared into the crowded salon.

"I really can't warm to that man," Jack stated, taking the now-vacant seat, setting the platter on top of the now-empty one. "See what delicacies I have brought you, ma'am?" He looked inordinately pleased with himself as he indicated the little salmon tartlets and caviar toast points. "And a footman is bringing us more champagne . . . ah, there he is." He waved at the man with a tray of glasses coming toward them.

Diana let Jack chatter, smiled her thanks for the fresh glass and absently took a tartlet, mainly to keep her escort happy.

"There you are, Diana, I've been looking all over for you." Fenella came up to her, her gown of bronze silk glimmering in the lamplight. "Oh, you found caviar." She took a toast point from the platter.

"Let me fetch you a chair, Fenella." Jack jumped to his feet and headed into the melee.

Fenella took his seat. "What's the matter, dearest? You've gone rather pale."

"Oh, it's nothing. It's hot in here, don't you find?"

Diana unfurled the delicate silk and ivory fan hanging from her wrist. "Too many people."

"It is quite a squeeze," Fenella agreed. "But it's unlike you to swoon from the heat."

Diana managed to laugh. "Of course I'm not swooning, goose. But I just had an encounter with a most disagreeable man. Do you know Lieutenant Colonel Cartwright?"

Fenella wrinkled her nose. "Only slightly, but he's such a cold fish. And so superior. He struts around as if he knows everything you don't."

"Exactly," Diana agreed. "He was at Mafeking, apparently."

"Oh." Fenella nodded her comprehension. "That explains it . . . why you're looking so out of sorts. What was he saying?"

That Rupert had not been there to stand by Jem.

Diana shook her head. "Nothing of any consequence. I'd just rather not be reminded of it, that's all." She took a sip of champagne. "How's Mark Singleton?"

Fenella shrugged. "He's always good company. In fact, he told me a fascinating story about—"

"I have another chair, but you ladies look so engrossed in conversation, perhaps I should take it and myself away." Jack's easy voice interrupted Fenella, who instantly stopped her tale.

"No, don't do that, Jack." She got to her feet. "I need to go to the cloakroom and make a few repairs. Please . . ." She gestured to her vacated chair. "I'll leave you and Diana to your delicacies." She picked up a tartlet, waved it cheerily at them, popped it in

her mouth and moved away, her silk skirts moving
fluidly with each step.

"So, Jack, tell me some gossip," Diana demanded,
trying to recapture her ordinary light and easy
manner.

Jack laughed. "Well, let me think . . ."

Rupert stood in the wide entrance to the salon,
surveying the scene. He saw Diana with Jack Marsden cozily ensconced in a niche on the far side of
the room. Diana was laughing at something Jack
had said, and she tapped his hand with her fan in an
intimately chiding gesture.

Rupert's expression darkened. There was nothing inappropriate in the way they were behaving,
but Diana's smile, her lightly graceful gestures redolent of easy familiarity and comfort in her escort's
company, twisted his gut. He could remember all
too vividly the time when she had eyes only for him,
when that easy, flirtatious intimacy was directed only
at him. In a crowded room, she would see no one
but him, and he would see only Diana, radiant, her
sloe eyes running over him, seeming to gather him
in to their own private orbit.

In the old days, she would have felt his arrival,
however far away he was, however many people
stood between them. Her eyes would have turned
instantly to him, her smile would have illuminated
her face and she would have left whoever she was
with and hurried to him, her hand outstretched,
careless of what anyone else might think about the
open, brazen delight she took in his presence. And

now she wasn't aware of him. She was engrossed in conversation with Marsden, her gaze intent on his face, her head slightly tilted to one side in a way Rupert watched with aching familiarity.

"Lacey, so glad you could come." His host pushed his way through the throng toward him. "Your charming wife said you were engaged with Roberts. Positive slave driver, I've heard. You should have sold out with the rest of us . . . well, most of us, at least. Cartwright and several others are furloughed, of course. Makes them difficult company." He clapped Rupert on the shoulder. "Come into the cardroom. There's a vicious game of whist going on, and I know for a fact that Dickie Edwards wants to yield his hand. You'd be welcome to take his place."

"In a minute, perhaps, Tim. I must first greet my wife."

"Yes, of course, dear fellow. Of course, one mustn't neglect the ladies." With another shoulder clap, Timothy Granger wandered away across the room toward the cardroom.

Rupert made his way to the niche where Diana sat, still engrossed in conversation with Jack. Her laughter greeted Rupert as he approached, a merry trill of genuine amusement he realized he hadn't heard in far too long.

"Something is amusing you, my dear," he observed lightly as he reached them. "Care to share it?" He nodded a greeting to Jack Marsden.

Diana looked up at him in surprise. "What are you doing here, Rupert? You said you weren't coming."

"I changed my mind. I trust my presence doesn't discommode you in any way." He raised an eyebrow just a fraction.

Diana flushed a little. "No, no, of course not. How could it? Won't you sit down?" She gestured to the third chair.

"Alas, no, I am expected at the whist table," he said smoothly. "But whenever you're ready to leave, let me know."

"There's no need for that. Jack will take me home," she said, frowning.

"I'm sure he would be more than happy to do so. Nevertheless, as I'm here, when you're ready to go home, let me know. I'll be more than ready to accompany you." He offered a benign smile to both of them and walked away to the cardroom.

Chapter Eighteen

"May I have this dance, Diana?" Tim Granger bowed gracefully as he extended an inviting hand. "It's the eightsome reel, and I have a particularly vivid memory of your dancing it one Christmas Eve with so much enthusiasm you lost your shoes."

Diana pulled a comical face. "Oh, I do remember that. One of them flew halfway across the dance floor. I'm much more restrained these days, you should know."

"Aren't we all?" Tim responded. "Set in our ways."

"Heaven forfend," Diana said. "Jack, you won't mind if I desert you for a reel?" She smiled with a quizzically raised brow.

"I do mind, but I cannot deprive our host of the company of the most beautiful woman in the room . . . excepting Mrs. Granger, of course," he added smoothly.

Diana went into a peal of laughter. "Nicely saved,

Jack." She gave her hand to her host as she rose to her feet and let him lead her onto the floor.

The movements of the reel were quite complicated and there was little opportunity for conversation between partners until the end. "I'm so thirsty," Diana said as the music ceased, fanning herself vigorously.

"Shall we sit the next one out?" Tim waved at a footman with his tray of glasses.

"Oh, but it's a military two-step," Diana said as the musicians struck up the first notes. She took a glass from the tray. "I can't resist that. A quick sip and then we'll dance."

Tim was more than willing, and when the vigorous two-step had yielded to the more sedate strains of a waltz, they stayed on the floor. "You were at Mafeking, weren't you?" Diana heard herself ask as she caught her breath.

"Yes, for my sins," her partner said. "Why?"

"Oh, no real reason. I suppose, because of my brother's death, I have an obsessive desire to hear all the details of the engagement."

"I don't remember much, except for the confusion and the noise," Tim said.

"Rupert says much the same. He can't seem to give me any details either."

"Was he there?" Tim frowned. "I suppose he must have been, but I don't recall seeing him. I saw your brother go down, and then it was hard to distinguish much of anything in the hand-to-hand melee."

Diana felt that chill again. Why had no one seen Rupert?

* * *

Rupert played whist for almost an hour, waiting with barely concealed impatience for Diana to signal that she was ready to leave. He caught glimpses of her now and again when he glanced up from his cards, casually looking through the arch into the main salon to the dance floor. She had been partnered by Tim Granger for three dances, and as the rubber came to an end, he pushed back his chair. "Gentlemen, thank you for the play, but I would like to dance with my wife. I've sadly neglected her."

"Mrs. Lacey doesn't seem at a loss for partners," one of his fellow players observed with a chuckle. "But then, Miss Sommerville was always the belle of the ball, as I recall."

Rupert smiled faintly. "I believe she was. If you'll excuse me." He rose to his feet with a gesture of farewell and made his way to the salon. He threaded his way through the dancing couples to Diana and her partner. He tapped Tim lightly on the shoulder. "May I cut in?"

"If you must," Tim said cheerfully. "I bow to a husband's prerogative. Thank you for your company, Diana." He stepped back as Rupert took his place.

"It's been a long time since we last danced together," Rupert observed softly. "But holding you like this, it seems only yesterday." Her body felt so familiar, her skin warm beneath the thin silk of her gown against his guiding hand in the small of her back. He breathed deeply of the vanilla scent of her hair, the delicate, flowery essence of her skin, and for a moment closed his eyes, concentrating on the flood of remembered sensations as she moved against him, as lithe and graceful as she had ever been.

Diana let the uncertainty and tension of her exchanges with Cartwright and Tim slide from her as she drifted into the past, where the feel of his hand on her back, the deft smoothness of his steps as they moved together, so in tune with each other, were as if they were one. All differences were banished, and all disagreements were mere bagatelles in the grand illusion of passion.

All too soon, it seemed, the music stopped, and the dancers broke apart. Rupert stepped back, his hands resting lightly on Diana's shoulders as he looked into her rapt countenance. "Shall we go home?"

She nodded, moistening her lips with the tip of her tongue. "I think we'd better." She looked around with a distracted air. "I should say good night to Jack."

"I think Jack can do without that courtesy just this once." Rupert took her hand. "Come." He drew her with him toward the gallery and the stairs.

They reached the head of the stairs just as Lieutenant Colonel Cartwright reached the top step from the hall below, a brandy glass in his hand. He paused on the step, essentially blocking their way. "Leaving so soon, Lacey? But with such a charming wife, who can blame you." His gaze flicked over Diana. "We were having a most interesting talk earlier about Mafeking." A thin smile touched his mouth as he stared at Rupert.

Diana felt Rupert stiffen beside her, but he merely said coldly, "Were you indeed?"

"Yes, most illuminating. Your wife seemed to have no details about the attack that killed her brother. She was under the impression you have no recall because it was dark when they charged. Oddly, I remember it as dawn, the sun coming up at the exact moment we engaged with the enemy. Maybe you were mistaken as to where you were at that moment?" He raised his glass in a sardonic toast and stepped aside to allow them passage.

Rupert's expression was hard as iron, his green eyes cold as jade. He said nothing at all, merely eased Diana in front of him on the stairs so she went down to the hall ahead of him. Diana said nothing either; she couldn't think of what to say. Cartwright was up to mischief with his sneering innuendo, that much was clear to her. And she would have dismissed it as jealous malice, except for Tim's uncertainty and Victor Marchant's comment. Neither of them had any reason to make up anything to do with Rupert and Jem.

A footman hurried to fetch a hackney for them as they stood in the hall, side by side and yet with a yawning gulf between them. If there was nothing to Cartwright's twisted tale, why didn't Rupert bring it up?

He handed her into the cab, and the silence between them continued on the drive back to Cavendish Square. Their earlier desire had vanished as if it had never been, and Diana wrapped herself in her fur stole and sank deeper into confused dismay. Rupert sat bolt upright against the squabs, his eyes on the middle distance, his expression closed in the way Diana knew all too well and dreaded.

When they reached Cavendish Square, he jumped down and extended a hand to Diana as she stepped to the pavement. Barlow let them in, and if he noticed the strained silence between them, he gave no indication.

"I think I'll go straight to bed," Diana said. "Good night, Rupert."

"Good night, Diana." He walked into the library, closing the door firmly behind him.

So what now? Diana went slowly upstairs, adrift in confusion and uncertainty.

She undressed, absently answering Agnes's questions about the evening, and climbed into bed with relief as Agnes left her. She sat propped up on her pillows, an open book neglected on her lap. Should she throw caution to the winds and ask Rupert directly where he'd been, what he'd been doing that dreadful dawn? But surely she should trust his word against that of a disgruntled fellow officer. Of course she should. But then, what about Tim and Victor Marchant and whoever had told him about Rupert's absence? None of them had an ax to grind.

Why did it matter? But of course it mattered. Rupert was enjoying the benefits of Jem's death. It was horrid to think of it like that, but Diana couldn't see any way around that conclusion. If Jem had not been killed, Rupert wouldn't be in possession of his fortune.

If it was true that Jem had made his will on the assumption he had years left to live and his sister would have a husband soon enough, that had backfired on that dreadful dawn. Suddenly, she set aside her book, threw off the covers and slid to the floor, reaching for her dressing gown. She couldn't go round and round like this for another minute. She would ask Rupert what Cartwright had meant. A simple request for clarification could not be construed as an accusation. It was surely only natural that she would be puzzled by his fellow officer's words.

The house was quiet, the servants gone to their own quarters. She ran downstairs, heedless of the chilly air on her bare feet. A light still shone under the library door. She opened it quietly. Rupert was sitting in an armchair, staring into the dying fire.

He looked up at the door's opening. "Diana, what on earth are you doing here? I thought you were going to bed."

"I have to talk to you." She closed the door behind her and came over to the fire, extending a bare foot to the residual warmth of the still-glowing embers. "That man, Cartwright. A thoroughly unpleasant man from what I could tell."

Rupert's expression didn't change. "I'll grant you that. Is he what you want to talk about?"

"Yes, well, not so much him as what he said. Why would he say you were not at Jem's side at Mafeking?"

"I can't imagine," Rupert said, his tone flat. "He is, as you say, a deeply unpleasant man. God only knows why he would want to stir up trouble. Why aren't you wearing slippers?"

"I forgot them." She brushed the question aside and warmed her other foot at the fire. "Does he bear you a grudge?"

Rupert shrugged. "Cartwright bears many people grudges. Including Jem," he added. "He decided he was passed over for promotion to full colonel because Jem had told the powers that be about a certain event that didn't show him in a good light."

"What event?" Diana was all curiosity now.

"It wasn't important, Diana. Just one of those things that blows up between bored men in close quarters and assumes an importance it doesn't warrant."

"Rupert, why must you talk in riddles?" she demanded impatiently. "Tell me what happened."

Rupert sighed, closing his eyes briefly. He had forgotten quite how persistent she could be . . . always had been, even as a child. "You're like a terrier with a bone," he said. "If you must know, Jem accused him of cheating at cards, and Cartwright challenged him to a duel. Duels," he added dryly, "are not approved of in the army."

"So Jem reported him?" Diana sounded incredulous. Jem would never tell tales.

"No, Jem did not. I did."

"*You.*" That was as extraordinary as if it had been her brother. "Why?"

"Because Jem intended to delope and assumed Cartwright would do the same, and honor would be satisfied. However, I was not as convinced as your brother that his opponent wouldn't kill him. So, I let it slip in certain places that there were suspicions that the lieutenant colonel had cheated. That was all it took. Cartwright was sent on a courier's errand to Ladysmith before any duel could take place, and Jem was promoted to full colonel. There, satisfied?"

"What a wretched story. Is that why he doesn't like you?"

Rupert shrugged again. "It's as good a reason as any. But I have absolutely no desire to be liked by the man, and I couldn't care less what he says." He stood up, reaching for her hands. "Shall we try to recapture our earlier mood?"

Diana wasn't sure she could, but it seemed churlish to deny him, so she smiled her assent, reaching against him as he brought his mouth to hers. And for a moment or two it seemed to her that everything was going to be all right. She slipped to the Aubusson carpet as he drew her down, reaching beneath her thin nightgown to caress her thighs and belly. She stirred beneath his stroking hand, unbuttoning his trousers, feeling for his erect sex.

But it wasn't all right. Instead of the familiar and glorious sensations of togetherness, the union of flesh that drove all else from her mind, she couldn't stop dwelling on the puzzle. It was like a persistent drumbeat at the forefront of her mind that drove out any other response. She tried; she tried to respond as Rupert expected, had every right to expect, but she couldn't find it, couldn't find the spark that would ignite the passionate dissolution her body craved. But she knew what it was supposed to feel like, knew what her responses should be, and she gave him what she knew he wanted. When it was over, she lay spread-eagled on the rug, her eyes closed, breathing quickly, waiting for his concluding kiss.

"Open your eyes, Diana."

Startled, she did so. He was kneeling over her, his expression impossible to read. "Don't you ever do that again."

"Do what?"

"You know what. If you don't want to make love, for whatever reason, you say so. Do you understand me?" He stood up, adjusting his dress, and reached down a hand to pull her to her feet.

Her nightgown fell back into place, brushing against her bare legs, fluttering against her ankles. She looked at him in silence, then asked, "How did you know?"

He gave a short, mirthless laugh. "Credit me with some sense. Do you really think I don't know your body well enough to know when you're pretending? Don't you really understand how insulting that little show was?"

"I didn't want to hurt you," Diana said. "I didn't mean to insult you, it was just . . . just . . ." The words died.

"Just what?"

He was angry, as angry as she had ever seen him, but it wasn't the kind of emotion she could meet and match because it was fueled by the hurt and confusion she had caused. "I don't know," she said eventually. "Forgive me."

He shook his head, not in denial but in acknowledgment of an impasse. "Go to bed, Diana. We won't talk of it again."

She hesitated, wanting something more, a kiss, a touch, something that affirmed his forgiveness, the renewal of their bond. But when he made no such move, she nodded and turned to the door. "Good night, Rupert."

"Good night, Diana."

Chapter Nineteen

Diana spent a wretched night, tossing and turning, tormented alternately with guilt and resentment. Guilt because she hadn't been honest with Rupert, and resentment because he hadn't been honestly forthcoming with her. She still hadn't asked him the question direct. *Was he there with Jem when her brother died?* And she was too afraid of his reaction to ask him.

There was a dull ache behind her temples and her eyes felt dry and sore. Perhaps a ride in the park would clear her head. She rang for Agnes and climbed out of bed, her muscles resisting vigorously. Perhaps she'd danced too much the previous evening. A ridiculous thought, of course. It wasn't possible to dance too much. She went into the bathroom to draw a bath.

"You're up and about bright and early, Miss Diana," Agnes observed, coming in with her morning tea. "Will you drink this in the bath?"

"Yes, thank you." Diana accepted the cup and

took a deep gulp. "I'm going for a ride before breakfast. Could you put out my habit?" She took another gulp, feeling marginally better as the hot, revivifying liquid burned its way down her throat. "And could you ask Billy to send a message to the mews to saddle Merry, please?"

Half an hour later, she was on her way downstairs when Rupert came in from outside, his complexion fresh from the early morning air, his eyes enviably clear and bright. He stopped in the hall, tapping his crop against his riding boot as he took in her appearance. "Going for a ride? It's chilly out there."

"I need the fresh air." Somehow, she couldn't arrange her features in an expression that seemed remotely normal, and it made her feel tongue-tied and awkward. She moved past him to the front door.

"Would you like some company?" he asked.

"But you've only just come in from a ride," Diana pointed out.

"Nevertheless, I'd be happy to accompany you if you'd like me to."

She swallowed. It sounded like an olive branch, and she wasn't going to wave it away. "If you really don't mind."

"No, I don't mind," he declared calmly but firmly, stepping ahead of her to open the door. "We'll walk round to the mews."

Hyde Park was quiet this early in the morning, and they met only a few other riders on the tan. Diana was not in the mood for conversation and Rupert, it seemed, was happy to maintain a companionable silence as they urged their mounts to a canter. After one circuit, they eased their horses to a walk alongside the Serpentine.

"Shall we stop for hot chocolate?" Rupert suggested, pointing to a small structure on the banks of the lake. "An enterprising couple have set up a little café over there."

"I never noticed that before." Diana turned Merry off the main ride and onto a narrow path across the grass down to the lake.

"It's a very recent innovation. But a welcome one, and a clever one too. The nursemaids and their charges will be out in force around midmorning and they're reliable customers." He turned his mount to follow her.

A few chairs were scattered on the grass in front of the shack, and Diana dismounted, fastening her reins to a conveniently placed hitching post. She looked out over the lake, gray under the cloudy September sky. In August it would have been busy with rowers and swimmers, women sheltering under wide-brimmed straw hats, young men handling the oars with various degrees of competence. The Serpentine was a truly egalitarian playground, attracting folk of every class on a Sunday, enjoying the freedom of a day of rest. Today it was deserted except for a trio of mute swans sedately paddling toward the bridge.

"Here you are, hot chocolate." Rupert emerged from the shack, carrying two steaming mugs. He handed one to Diana and lightly clinked his own against hers in a mock toast. She sipped the rich, dark, sweet brew. "Do they have a Primus stove?"

"Several," he answered.

A strained silence fell, far from their earlier companionable quiet. Diana knew the strain was coming from her; she could feel the need for answers bubbling within her until it could no longer be contained.

"Were you really at Jem's side at Mafeking?"

"What?" He looked at her, his green gaze incredulous. "What are you asking me?"

"If you were at Jem's side when he was killed." She averted her gaze as she spelled it out finally, resigned now to whatever was going to happen. She needed the truth more than she needed peace with Rupert. The latter was not possible without the former.

When he said nothing, she continued slowly, still without looking at him, "I can discount Cartwright's malice, but Tim Granger said he didn't see you there, and Victor Marchant, the agent in Kimberley, said it was common knowledge you hadn't been beside Jem during the attack, and he said everyone was surprised at your absence. So, I'm asking if you *were* there, because if you were, I don't understand why all these people believe you weren't." Her eyes remained on the dull gray lake and the white swans.

Rupert turned away from her, his own gaze seeking the peaceful anonymity of the lake. His mind had gone back to that morning on the 12th of May, two years earlier.

They heard them before they saw them in the pitch-dark moments before the African dawn. A rustle in the bush, a hiss that could have been a whisper, and they smelled the smoke. The shouts and yells of triumph came a few minutes later, lifting goose bumps on the back of his neck. He knew what was happening: after seven months of siege, the town of Mafeking was under attack. The Boer farmers outnumbered the British garrison seven to one and the surprise attack had caught them off guard.

Jem raised his rifle to his shoulder. He squinted through the dark and smoke. "Can you see anything, Rupert?"

"Not yet." Rupert, standing next to him in the line, spoke curtly, trying to make out any shape in the obscurity ahead. Behind them, their fellow soldiers moved into readiness to meet the oncoming assault, but there were only ten of them, and they knew the odds were way against them.

"The gunpowder," Rupert murmured to Jem. "The damn gunpowder. We have to do something."

"Where are the police reinforcements from the village?" Jem muttered as if he hadn't heard his friend.

Rupert crept swiftly away from the line at the front of the redoubt, his one thought to get to the pile of ordnance in the makeshift shed behind the redoubt. It was packed with gunpowder, and if it went up, the entire garrison would go up with it.

The smoke came from the thatched huts in the village that housed the native African troops just beyond the garrisoned walls of Mafeking. Something flew past his ear with a nasty whine. Behind him, someone cursed and slapped at his neck as if at a mosquito.

And then the sun came up, a great golden ball in the African sky, and the enemy came out of the dawn, bayonets fixed, rifles blazing, and for a disbelieving moment it seemed to the British soldiers they were facing the entire Boer army in this one little place. Rupert hesitated. Jem was in the front line, his place was beside him, but if a stray spark caught the explosives, the entire garrison would be massacred. He ducked low and ran to the shed. Behind him, the sounds of shots, screams, the war cries in the attackers' barbaric Afrikaans tongue bombarded him as he hurled buckets of water from the line kept as a precaution outside the shed, drenching the gunpowder, desperate to render it useless before the attackers breached the front line.

He could only imagine the chaos in the redoubt, but he had one task to do. Jem was an excellent shot, he told himself. But he didn't see the moment the giant figure flung himself at Jem with a great bellow. And afterward he could only imagine what went through Jem's mind as he realized that Rupert, his oldest and closest friend, his comrade in arms, was not beside him. He could only imagine what happened when the giant Dutchman came down on him, Jem trying to roll sideways away from the thrusting bayonet, no one to support him, to fight for him because in that ghastly melee every man fought for himself. He could only imagine what it must have felt like as the enemy's vicious point plunged into Jem's body beneath his right arm and the darkness engulfed him.

* * *

"I carried Jem's body to the rear," he said finally, his voice without expression. "I tried to staunch his wound, but there was nothing to be done." He turned back to his horse. "I trust that satisfies your curiosity."

Diana had no words against the wall he had thrown up, the wall she had experienced before on the banks of the Orange River. She had questioned his word, his honor, whatever it was Rupert held so dear, and now she would pay the price. *And it wasn't just.* She wanted to scream the words at him, to penetrate the wall, but she couldn't.

They rode home in silence, leaving their horses in the mews. "I'm going to Horse Guards. Can you take yourself back to the house?"

"Yes, of course." Diana watched him stride out of the mews, a great emptiness in her heart. He had been there, whatever others might say. And she had doubted him.

She went back to the house and was wrestling with the household accounts when Fenella and Petra were announced. She greeted the diversion with relief. "Are you feeling better, Petra?"

"Much. I discovered whiskey, honey and lemon," Petra said cheerfully. "It's a miracle cure. What are you doing?"

"Accounts. Cameron's stable bill is huge, but I suppose that's only to be expected with a Thoroughbred." She closed the books decisively. "So, anything interesting to impart?"

"Not really." Fenella drew off her gloves and

tossed them onto a table. "We came to persuade you to come to Fortnum's for lunch."

It was the last thing Diana felt like doing, but it would take her mind off the morning and maybe give her some space to decide how she was to face Rupert. She was determined not to let silence rule again. He had to accept that she had had legitimate concerns, and they warranted an answer. It wasn't as if she had actually accused him of anything.

She returned to Cavendish Square in the late afternoon, determined to have it out with Rupert as soon as he returned, but when she walked into the house she knew something was wrong. It was in the air, an unsettled feeling. Barlow's expression was a study in neutrality, which in itself was unusual. He always had a smile and a pleasant greeting.

"Will you let me know when Colonel Lacey returns, please?" she asked, heading for the stairs.

Barlow coughed. "Colonel Lacey left some two hours ago, Miss Diana."

She spun around, a prickle of foreboding on the back of her neck. "Did he say when he would be back?"

"No, ma'am. He left a letter for you in your parlor." The butler coughed into his gloved hand. "He took rather a lot of luggage, so I would imagine he was expecting to be away for some time."

Diana felt the color drain from her cheeks and she turned hastily back to the stairs lest Barlow see her dismay. "I expect he explains it in his letter," she said, trying to sound nonchalant. "Lord Roberts has probably sent him on a mission of some kind."

"Yes, I'm sure that's so, Miss Diana."

Diana ran upstairs and along to her parlor. The letter, in its white envelope with the familiar black script, seemed to shout at her from the escritoire. She picked it up carefully, as if it would burn her fingers, and sliced through the seal with the dainty silver paper knife. Slowly, she unfolded the single sheet.

My dear Diana, I yield. You're right that it's not possible for us both to live under the same roof. Both Jem and I had hoped that maybe proximity would naturally lead us back to the time when we loved and trusted each other. But I realize it was a fool's hope. So I leave you in possession of the field, my dear. I have talked to Muldoon and explained the situation. He will handle my financial interests from your brother's inheritance and you will not be troubled. As far as the world is concerned you may say that I have gone abroad. I'll come up with a more permanent arrangement and explanation in a few weeks. R.

She read and reread the letter. She could hear his hurt and anger in every syllable. He had given her what she had wanted, what she had fought for with increasing frustration. But she didn't want it. Not anymore.

Talk about a Pyrrhic victory. She flung herself down on the couch, the letter still in her hand. What did he mean about Jem, that he had hoped proximity would bring them back together? Was that why Jem had left his inheritance to Rupert?

It seemed obvious now. It was so typical of her brother. He had never made any secret of his sorrow and disappointment that his beloved sister and his greatest friend would not, after all, make a match. Jem would always do everything he could to achieve a desired object, and in this case, he'd made provision in the event he couldn't bring about that object himself. What would be more natural in Jem's view than if the two of them were thrown together, forced to negotiate; they would once again find that passionate connection.

And they had come so close . . . so very close.

Where would Rupert have gone? He had friends, colleagues from the regiment, but knowing him as she did, she couldn't imagine him seeking help from anyone. It wasn't in his nature. Rupert wasn't like other people. Whenever he was hurt as a boy, he would hide it, would go off on his own, and she and Jem had learned to leave him alone until he had healed himself. He would be licking his wounds now, somewhere alone.

No, no, no. Not this time. She scrunched up the letter and hurled it against the far wall. She was not going to let him hide, dwelling on the angry resentment gnawing at him. This time she needed to find him, to compel him to let her in, to help her understand what caused him to withdraw at the slightest hint of mistrust. She accepted he was hurt, and that without intention she had inflicted that hurt. With or without just cause, she *had* caused him pain.

So she must help him heal, but she had to fight her own battle too. There could be no future for them on Rupert's terms alone. Diana knew now that a future with Rupert was the only one she could contemplate. He was an impossible, controlling, stubborn man, but they shared a passion for each other that transcended ordinary emotions. He understood her as only Jem had, and she understood all his contradictions, except for this one puzzling obsession.

But before there could be talk of a future, she had to find him. Where would he have gone?

Deerfield, perhaps? She considered this possibility and then dismissed it as too obvious. Perhaps he had really gone abroad. That was a depressing possibility. Abroad was a big place. He'd presumably obtained a leave of absence from Lord Roberts. Perhaps they knew at Horse Guards where he'd gone. But she could hardly go there and ask if they knew where her husband was. The gossip would spread like wildfire.

And then it came to her with absolute certainty. Rupert would have gone to his estate in Yorkshire. On his grandfather's death several years earlier, he had inherited the estate, but the place held such grim memories for him, he never visited if he could help it. But his former mistress was still there, still able to offer him comfort, presumably. He was still in touch with her, still gave her money; he had said as much.

Diana swallowed the unpalatable image of Rupert taking comfort in the arms of Margery Ordway. It was silly to let her imagination run wild, she told herself firmly. There was no reason to suppose any such thing.

Thwaite. That was the town. The Lacey estate was outside Thwaite. So how did one get to Thwaite? She needed a *Baedekers*, and there was a copy of the traveler's bible in the library. With a surge of energy, Diana flew downstairs to the library. But in the doorway, she stopped. Rupert permeated the room, the sense of his presence almost overwhelming. She could smell the stuff of his uniform, the tonic he used on his hair, the freshness of his skin. The image of him sitting at the big table as she had so often found him filled her with longing. How could she have wanted so desperately to get him out of her house, out of her life?

Resolutely, she put all such useless thoughts behind her and went unerringly to the shelf where she would find *Baedekers*. She took down the red leather volume and carried it to the table, skimming the index until she found Thwaite in the Yorkshire Dales. It looked to be in the middle of nowhere, but Mr. Muirhead M.A., who had compiled the travel guide, had not been troubled by something as unimportant as *nowhere*. He described exactly how to get there, which trains to take and which hotels would be most suitable for a lady traveling alone.

Diana drew a sheet of paper toward her, dipped the pen nib in the inkwell and began to write, copying Mr. Muirhead's directions. She would change trains at Kendal for the branch line to Hawes Junction. She would leave the train there and spend the night at the King's Arms, which was considered a suitably decorous hostelry for a single lady. Presumably, they would have a horse and trap, which would take her to Thwaite, or rather to Lacey Manor.

Satisfied, Diana closed the book and returned it to its shelf. Then she went to her bedroom to instruct Agnes about packing for her journey to the Yorkshire Dales.

Agnes didn't hide her surprise at Diana's instructions. "It's a rough part of the world from all I hear, Miss Diana. Full of sheep and hills, and the folk speak a different language. Why do we want to go there?"

"*We* don't, Agnes," Diana replied. "I'm going alone."

"Dear Lord, not if I have anything to say about it," Agnes protested, reverting to her nursemaid ways. "A young girl alone in those wilds. Lord only knows what the folk are like up there, but stands to reason they'll not be like any you're used to."

"Nevertheless, Agnes dear, I intend to go alone. I'm not exactly a young girl anymore and I will be quite safe, *Baedekers* tells me so." She flourished her sheet of written directions. "Besides, I'm rather assuming Colonel Lacey will be there, so you need have no fears for my safety."

Agnes didn't look mollified. She sniffed her disapproval and said, "You'll be needing warm clothes. Are you taking the dogs?"

"No, I can't manage them on such a long journey. I'll have to change trains several times."

"Well, on your own head be it," Agnes declared.

"What your sainted mother would say, I really don't know."

Neither did Diana, but she kept a prudent silence, acceding meekly to Agnes's statement that she'd find her dinner in her parlor, and she'd best get to bed early if she was to make an early start the next morning.

Chapter Twenty

Diana stepped off the train at Hawes Junction carrying only a small valise. It had been chilly in London, but the north wind here in the Yorkshire Dales bit like a knife, slicing through her fur-trimmed coat. The platform was unsheltered and deserted, but the station manager's cottage stood at the end of the platform, where a narrow lane led somewhere . . . the town of Hawes, she supposed. Diana made her way to the building, where someone had made an effort to create a garden that could survive the bitter wind. She was unlatching the gate when the front door opened and a rotund gentleman in a stationmaster's uniform, his tunic undone, his shirt collar somewhat grubby, stepped out onto the path clutching a napkin, with which he hastily wiped his mouth.

"Beg pardon, ma'am. I didn't expect anyone off the seven thirty. Most folk don't get out 'ere after the afternoon train's passed."

"No, I can see why not." Diana shivered at a renewed gust of wind whistling around the corner of the cottage. She was exhausted after traveling since early that morning, changing trains several times and now finding herself in this bleak spot, desperate for a warm bed and a hot supper. "Can you tell me how to get to the King's Arms in Hawes?"

The man looked a little doubtful. "'Tis late, ma'am."

"Yes, I am aware," she returned more sharply than she'd intended. "But I don't intend to spend the night on this drafty platform. So there must be some form of transport available."

"Aye, well, there's the gig. 'Appen I could drive you to the King's Arms if'n ye'd like."

Diana squashed a sardonic retort and forced a smile. "I'd be most grateful, Mr. . . . ?"

"Garth's the name, ma'am. Ye'd best come in out o' the cold while I get the gig." He gestured behind him to the cottage door.

"Thank you, Garth." Diana stepped eagerly into the small living room where a woodstove burned, sending out welcome warmth. She stood in front of it, warming her icy hands. The last train on the branch line to Hawes hadn't been heated and she was half frozen.

No wonder Rupert referred to his native land as a godforsaken tundra most of the time, she reflected, blowing on her hands as she rotated her body in front of the heat.

"Right y'are, then. Gig's ready," the stationmaster announced from the door, and Diana forced herself away from the warmth and out into the cold evening.

The gig was open to the elements, but the ancient nag between the shafts seemed to be as eager as its passenger to reach its destination and set off at a brisk trot.

The King's Arms was an old coaching inn standing at the crossroads in the center of a sleepy, gray-stone village. The windows were lit, which was a good sign, Diana thought thankfully. She'd been beginning to wonder if she'd find any shelter in this alien countryside. It was so different from the soft, gently rolling hills of her native Kent.

The stationmaster pulled up the gig on the road outside the inn. "'Ere you be, then." He didn't attempt to get down from his perch to help her, so she half-jumped, half-stepped to the street, reaching in to grab her bag. "What do I owe you?"

He shrugged. "Sixpence 'll do, I reckon."

Diana fumbled in her change purse, found only a shilling and handed it to him. "Thank you."

"Can't give ye no change."

"I don't expect any." She raised a hand in farewell and carried her bag into the inn. Voices and the sound of a fiddle came from the taproom to one side of the narrow stone-flagged passageway. At least the place was open and hospitable. Diana pushed open the door onto the crowded taproom and blinked in the fug of pipe smoke and gusting smoke from the fire as the wind rattled in the chimney. She wrinkled her nose at the reek of stale beer and sweat, but at least it was warm. All eyes were on her as she stepped in, closing the door quickly behind her to keep out the drafts. Silence fell.

"Eh, lass, what's one like ye doin' 'ere?" The

question came from a ruddy-cheeked woman swathed in a coarse apron. "We wasn't expectin' no one."

"No, of course not. But I just got off the train at Hawes Junction and *Baedekers* said you had rooms for travelers."

"Oh, aye, that we do, but we don't get many of 'em once summer's been an' gone," the woman declared cheerfully. "But if you've a mind to it, I've a chamber above that might suit ye." She bustled past Diana, out into the passage again. "Reckon it'll be a bit parky, like, but I'll get the girl to light the fire while you 'ave a bite o' supper downstairs." She looked at Diana somewhat critically before climbing a narrow, creaking staircase. "There's a small parlor at back, but 'tis chilly, although there's a bit of a fire there. Reckon you'll not want to sup in the taproom wi' all that noise, an' the men can be a bit rough."

"The taproom will be fine, Mrs. . . . ?"

"Clavell, ma'am. Well, if'n y'are sure." On the landing, the innkeeper opened a wooden door with a sloping lintel. "This do ye?"

It was a small, sparsely furnished dormer room, but it was clean with a bed, a washstand and a fireplace, at present cold and empty. "Yes, thank you, Mrs. Clavell. It will do me nicely." Diana set her valise on the bed.

"I'll send up Tabby to see t' the fire. It'll warm up in no time, an' she'll put a hot-water bottle in the bed. Make yerself at 'ome an' come down when y'are ready. There'll be a good meat pie an' tatties an' a nice drop of porter to warm ye."

"Sounds heavenly," Diana said with perfect truth. The prospect of a thick feather mattress with a hot-water bottle was so wonderful, she would almost have foregone the pie and potatoes, but she was very hungry.

She was tidying herself up when a girl came in with a coal scuttle and an armful of kindling. She nodded shyly at Diana and knelt to light the fire. The spurt of flame and the crackle of wood ushered Diana downstairs for her supper. This time when she entered the taproom, no one took any notice of her except the landlady, who pointed her to a small table set in an alcove by the fire.

She set a laden plate with a massive slice of meat pie, its crust golden and glistening, and a mountain of potato in front of her guest with a basket of fresh bread and a large tankard of porter. "There now, get that down ye," she instructed. "And don't pay no mind to that lot." She gestured with her chin to the room's occupants.

Diana smiled and took a draft from her tankard, relishing the earthy jolt as the strong ale slipped down her throat. It wasn't a drink she was accustomed to, but it seemed entirely appropriate in present circumstances and certainly seemed to suit the food. Her companions in the taproom seemed amiable enough, although they ignored her for the most part, but she was in no mood for conversation. Only when she'd finished her supper and the landlady came to take her plate did she ask, "Do you know how I might find Lacey Manor? It's outside Thwaite, I believe."

The woman looked at her in surprise, and the voices in the taproom died down. "Aye, 'tis about ten miles from 'ere. Miserable place 'tis, if'n ye ask me."

"Aye, old man Lacey was a misery an' a half," one of the men said, blowing a puff of smoke into the fug.

"I understand his grandson inherited the estate," Diana said.

"Aye, that poor lad," the innkeeper said. "'Twas no way for a child t' live, all alone in that great 'ouse with only the old man for company."

"I believe Colonel Lacey is at the house now," Diana ventured.

The woman shrugged. "Wouldn't know nowt about that, lass. Us folk keep ourselves to ourselves an' he didn't pass through 'ere."

Diana told herself not to be discouraged. There was no reason to expect that Rupert would have made exactly the same journey she had. She gave a vague smile, repeating, "How would I get there in the morning?"

"Oh, our Jack'll take ye in the cart. He's goin' over Buttertubs Pass to the sheep market in Thwaite. If ye don't mind sharin' the cart with the lambs."

"No, no, of course I don't mind," Diana answered the speaker, a sturdy, broad-shouldered man with a thick black beard. "I'd be most grateful."

"Early start then," the man said, draining his tankard. "Our Jack'll be by aroun' six."

"I'll be ready," Diana promised.

She took her leave of the taproom soon after and found her chamber warm from a blazing fire, softly lit by candles on the mantel, a jug of hot water and an ewer on the washstand. Mr. Muirhead M.A. hadn't been wrong, although she wasn't sure how many single ladies of a certain decorum had actually stayed here. She blew out the candles and fell into the deep featherbed, curling herself around the stone hot-water bottle, considerately covered in a knitted cover. Tomorrow would bring what tomorrow would bring.

Tomorrow brought the girl, Tabby, with a jug of hot water and an enormous cup of strong, brick-red tea. "Mistress says yer breakfast'll be in t' taproom in ten minutes."

"Thank you." Diana yawned and forced her reluctant eyes to open on a gray dawn. The fire had gone out overnight and the room was cold. She leaped out of bed, washed her face and dressed rapidly, shivering all the while. A glance out of the small window showed her a fog-wreathed landscape of fields stretching into the mist.

She hurried downstairs to the taproom, stale-smelling from old pipe smoke and spilled beer, but blessedly warm from a massive log fire in the inglenook. Mrs. Clavell set before her a steaming bowl of porridge with a jug of thick yellow cream. "There's bacon, eggs, an' black puddin' to follow."

Diana smiled her thanks, poured cream and brown sugar liberally into her porridge bowl and took up her spoon. It occurred to her that she had no way of knowing when she would eat again that day, so she'd best make the most of the moment. If she had guessed wrong and Rupert wasn't at Lacey Manor, she had no idea what she would do. Better not to be defeatist, she told herself firmly, and applied herself to her breakfast, carefully avoiding the black pudding.

Jack appeared with the cart on the dot of six o'clock. Diana paid the landlady and climbed up next to the driver on the bench seat. The small flock of lambs crated in one corner of the rear of the open cart greeted her with pathetic bleats.

"There's a 'orse blanket somewhere," Jack told her as she established herself beside him, her valise at her feet. "Like as not ye'll be needin' it up on the pass. Wind's fearful cold up there."

The horse blanket reeked of horse and other unsavory, unidentifiable substances, but Diana was not too fastidious to take advantage of its warmth. And she was more than glad of it as they climbed Buttertubs Pass. The morning mist had cleared, and from the top of the pass Diana took in the patchwork tapestry of fields below, bisected with low stone walls, dotted with sheep and cattle. Smoke rose from the chimneys of scattered hamlets and lone farmhouses. On a warm summer day it would have been beautiful, but the sun was not yet up, and on a freezing autumn morning, it was more desolate than anything.

"Can we see Lacey Manor from here, Jack?"

The boy half-turned on his bench, pointing with his whip. "Over yonder, miss. That gray 'ouse with all them trees. The 'ome farm's just be'ind it. Rest of the cottages are all tenant farmers. Old man Lacey, beggin' yer pardon, miss, didn't do nothin' for 'is tenants. Let them cottages go to rack and ruin."

"What's happened to them since he died?" Diana asked, leaning closer to hear him better over the wind.

"The colonel sacked the old agent and put in a new bloke. Been a bit better since." He craned his neck to look at her more closely. "We don't get strangers much up 'ere. You got business at the manor?"

"I'm not sure" was the only vaguely truthful answer Diana could come up with.

Jack nodded rather doubtfully, observing, "Not known fer likin' visitors much, there."

Diana made no response, holding on to the side of the cart as it began the steep descent to the valley. Behind her, the lambs continued their mournful bleating from their crate.

It was a little warmer in the valley and the sun was up now. Diana looked around her with growing interest and growing apprehension. What if Rupert was not there? What if he refused to see her?

When Jack turned the cart onto a long, rutted driveway leading up to the gray-stone manor, Diana was a bundle of nerves. The house seemed dark and deserted. The windows were all closed, no light or life showing behind the grimy panes. A trickle of smoke came from one of the chimneys, but other than that, the place seemed uninhabited.

"You sure you want me to leave ye 'ere, miss?" Jack helped her down from the cart and set her valise on the ground at her feet.

"Yes, quite sure, Jack," she said with a confidence she didn't feel.

"Well, per'aps I'll stop by on my way back from market," he suggested. "Just in case ye need a ride back to the King's Arms."

Diana felt a surge of relief. "Thank you, that would be wonderful, if it's not too much trouble."

"Nay, no trouble. I'll be passin' by about five. Need to get back over the pass afore dark." He touched his cap and climbed back onto the bench, taking up the reins. "Come on, then, Betsy girl." He flicked the reins, and the horse started back up the driveway.

Diana watched them go, then she picked up her bag and approached the door. There was no bellpull, only a massive brass ring. She lifted it and banged it down as hard as she could. Nothing happened, and there was no sound from within. She tried again, this time banging it twice in succession. Still nothing.

Picking up her bag, she set off around the house to see if there was any life at the rear. A weed-tangled gravel path circled the building, and she paused now and again to peer through a window into the gloomy interior. The windows were too dirty to provide much visibility, and gradually, the sensation of walking around a ghost house crept up on her. If Rupert was in residence, surely there would be some sign of life.

She rounded the corner and found herself in a courtyard with outhouses and stables. Chickens clucked and pecked across the cobbles and the rain butts were full. Piglets squealed and snorted, pushing one another to get at the trough, which was filled with swill. It was a working farmyard, which meant someone had to be around.

Diana was conscious of the muck underfoot, the cobbles encrusted with dung and straw. She looked at the back of the manor house, where a door stood open onto the yard. Rather tentatively, she took a step toward the open door just as a woman appeared, staring at Diana with a degree of hostility.

"Aye, ye be wantin' summat?"

The woman was older than Diana, but still young, and if her face had not been so drawn, set in such hard lines and her expression less suspicious, she would have been pretty. Her hair was scraped into a bun beneath a kerchief, her thin frame swathed in a striped apron.

"I was hoping to see Colonel Lacey," Diana said, feeling her courage return as she looked directly at the woman. She was not going to be outfaced by a farmer's wife. "I understood he was here."

"Who wants 'im?"

"I don't believe that's your business," Diana said steadily, meeting the hostile stare head-on. "Could you tell me if he's here, please?"

"The colonel don't want no visitors."

"I think you'll find he'll want to see me."

For a moment, it felt to Diana as if they were two bull dogs facing each other across a disputed bone, and suddenly it came to her. "I beg your pardon, Mrs. . . . ? Are you by any chance Margery Ordway?"

There was a subtle change in the woman's demeanor. "An' what if I am?"

Diana turned the full bore of her smile on her antagonist and stepped forward, extending her hand. "Rupert has told me so much about you. You mean so much to him. I am Diana Sommerville. He may have mentioned me?"

"Aye, 'appen he has, once or twice." Margery still looked a little suspicious, but the rigidity had left her. "He didn't tell me 'e was expectin' ye."

"No, because he wasn't . . . isn't," Diana told her with a disarming smile. "But I have a very important message for him."

"Oh, aye?" Margery didn't make any move, welcoming or otherwise.

"Is he in the house?" Diana asked, trying to control her impatience.

"Nay, Rupert's gone to east field. A ewe got caught in t' fence."

Diana was not surprised Rupert was doing farmwork; he and Jem had often worked on the home farm at Deerfield, and frequently turned their hands to stable work in Kimberley. Her father had insisted his son embrace the life of a gentleman farmer as an antidote to the dilettante existence of a scion of a privileged and wealthy family. And as far as Rupert was concerned, Sir Geoffrey had decided that because he had lineage and status but no fortune, it was as well he learned to turn his hand to practical matters. Rupert and Jem had loved every minute of their farming education. Infinitely more than the lessons Harrow had taught them.

"Then I'll wait for him. May I wait inside?"

"Aye, nowt t' do wi' me," Margery replied, indicating the open door. "Kitchen fire's goin'."

"Thank you." Diana walked into the kitchen. It was a typical farm kitchen, but rather to her surprise it was clean, the red-flagged floor shining, the pewter pots gleaming, the range glowing. She sat in a rocking chair by the range, set her valise at her feet and wondered what to do next. What she really wanted to do was explore the house, this mausoleum where

Rupert had spent so many miserable years of his early childhood. Would he consider it prying?

Margery was peeling apples at the scrubbed pine table, ignoring Diana, and after a moment, Diana got up. "I'm going to take a walk around the house," she announced, hoping to convey in her tone the fact that her relationship with the master of the house meant she was entitled to go where she pleased.

Margery merely shrugged. "Best take a lamp wi' ye, then. 'Tis dark and the stairs are uneven. Take care ye don't break a leg."

"I will. Thank you." Diana took up an oil lamp, lit a taper in the range and touched the wick. Yellow light flared. Holding the lamp high, she left the brightness of the kitchen and stepped out into the interior of the house.

Chapter Twenty-One

The cold hit her the minute she left the warmth of the kitchen behind. She found herself in a narrow passageway, stone-flagged with rough, whitewashed walls. It opened into a square hall, furnished with an oak chest and a bench by the door, where one could remove outdoor footwear. The chill felt old, as if the very air had been stagnating in the enclosed space. The front door was barred and bolted and didn't look as if it had ever been opened. Two doors on either side of the front door revealed a dining room and a parlor, both dusty and neglected.

Diana shivered, turning up the fur collar of her coat as she drew the coat closer around her. She turned to the staircase, which rose into darkness, and went up hesitantly. A window on the landing at the top was shuttered, which explained the darkness. Decisively, she unlatched the shutters and threw them open. The morning light showed her a square landing, two passages leading off it. The walls were paneled in heavy oak, and wide oak planks

were underfoot, all of which added to the gloom.
The air was as cold and stale as it was downstairs.

Where did Rupert sleep? She held her lamp higher,
throwing yellow beams along the passages in turn.
She headed down the east passage, opening doors
as she went. They all gave onto bedrooms, dark paneled with heavy furniture, massive armoires and
four-poster beds and threadbare rugs on the oak
floors. None of them seemed to have been inhabited in recent memory.

At the end of the passage, there was another shuttered window, and Diana wrestled with the shutters,
which were stiff, as if they hadn't been opened in
years. Probably hadn't, she reflected, finally getting
them open. The window looked out onto fields and
hills in the distance. She retraced her steps and ex-
plored the second passage. This was much the same
as the first, except that the last bedroom was occupied, and its window was unshuttered. It was smaller
than any of the others she had seen. The narrow cot
was made up with a thick checkered quilt, towels
hung on the washstand, and Rupert's clothes hung
in the wardrobe. It was as cold as everywhere else,
gray ashes in the fireplace.

Diana stood in the doorway, feeling the desola-
tion of the mean little chamber. Had this been
Rupert's childhood bedroom? Was that why he was
sleeping here now, when there were other spacious
bedrooms that could be made comfortable with a
little effort?

He'd been four years old when his parents had
died of typhus. She tried to imagine what it must
have been like for that small boy, grieving for his

parents, not really knowing what had happened, finding himself in this desolate place with a grandfather he had described as taciturn, ill-tempered, morose, with no time at all for his little grandson, who'd been left to his own devices until he was six and could be sent away to school.

How hard it must have been for Rupert to learn to love, when he'd never experienced love himself until he'd found himself in the midst of her own welcoming and gregarious family. But despite the warm acceptance of the Sommervilles, that childhood abandonment must have run deep. So deep that maybe he felt he couldn't truly trust in the permanence of the Sommerville affection.

Did that mean, then, that when Diana questioned his truths it had seemed to him that she didn't trust him? And if she didn't trust him, how could he be certain of her love? He had always been a complicated person to understand, Diana had always acknowledged that, but until now, standing in the doorway of this miserable bedroom, she hadn't fully realized why.

She shook her head with a sigh of frustration. Even if she now understood him better, even if she could make excuses for him, it still wasn't right that he should have everything on his terms. He had hurt her too, by putting the worst interpretation on her questions and by cutting himself off so completely. She couldn't possibly live with a man who would not permit her to ask questions, to seek explanations, who demanded absolute acceptance of his needs without any understanding of hers.

Diana turned away, closing the door behind her, and made her way back to the landing. She wondered whether to close the shutters and then decided against it. It was high time to let light into this gloom. She went back to the kitchen and then stopped at the sound of raised voices from the yard beyond the open door.

A man was shouting, a woman shrieking. They didn't seem to be speaking English, Diana thought, straining to hear what was being yelled. She had enough trouble deciphering the near-impenetrable Yorkshire accent, but these sounds seemed to be a dialect that bore little or no relation to the English tongue as Diana understood it.

The woman's shrieks became frantic, and Diana ran across the kitchen to the door. A massive man with hands like hams was dragging Margery by the hair across the yard toward the pig trough. She was fighting, trying to dig her heels into the cobbles, but his grip on her hair was too strong. Diana remembered Rupert saying that Margery's husband was a violent brute, just as her father had been. Without a second thought, she grabbed a pail of water standing by the door and ran across the yard, hurling it at the man. It hit him full in the face and he bellowed like an enraged bull, dropping his hold on Margery's hair and spinning to face his assailant, water dripping from his head. He lunged for Diana, who danced nimbly out of reach.

Margery, who had received a fair share of the bucket of water, shook her head, her hands massaging her dripping scalp. Then she ran for the kitchen, while Diana ducked and dodged the huge hands reaching for her. It was barely midmorning, but the man reeked of whiskey. Out of the corner of her eye, she caught sight of a broom leaning against the wall of the outhouse. Turning, she ran for it, grabbing it up and swinging it wildly as she twisted to face the man. The stick caught him across the cheek, and he let loose a stream of vile oaths before she swung it again, catching him on the other cheek. He lowered his head, shaking it like a charging bull, and Margery hit him squarely on the head with a heavy cast-iron skillet. Diana watched, fascinated, as he dropped slowly to one knee, still shaking his lowered head. She swung her broomstick again, catching him across the ear, and he went down to the cobbles, crumpling like an empty paper sack.

Diana began to laugh, and after a moment, Margery joined her as they stood over their fallen assailant. "Dear God, is he your husband?" Diana asked through her laughter, which had an edge of hysteria to it.

"Aye, an' he'll be ragin' mad when 'e comes to," Margery said, wiping her eyes with a corner of her apron.

"Bravo, ladies." Rupert's voice seemingly came out of nowhere. Diana turned at the sound. Rupert strode across the yard, clapping his hands in slow rhythm. "That was quite a fight you both put up." He stopped and looked down disdainfully at the fallen man. "What d'you want to do with him, Margery? Shall I throw him in the duck pond?"

Diana looked at him, thinking distractedly how

different he looked. He wore a collarless shirt with a loosely tied scarf at the throat, leather britches and a leather jerkin, boots that were scuffed and muddy. His copper hair was tousled, unruly curls flopping over his broad forehead. And she didn't think she had ever seen him look more desirable.

"Just leave 'im," Margery said. "'E'll sleep it off where 'e lies. Reckon he'll 'ave quite a 'ead on him when 'e wakes."

"Sure about the duck pond?" Rupert asked wistfully.

Margery chuckled. She glanced shrewdly between Rupert and Diana. "Reckon as you two 'ave summat to talk about. I'll be off 'ome, then. There's a fresh lardy cake in t' pantry." She nodded at Diana. "My thanks. Silas would 'ave 'ad me in the pig trough wi'out you."

"It was my pleasure," Diana replied with absolute sincerity. Margery nodded again and left the yard.

"What are you doing here, Diana?" Rupert asked, keeping his distance, his voice even, giving no indication of his reaction to her appearance.

"I wanted an explanation," she responded, wishing he would put an arm around her, touch her in some way. "You disappeared without a word—"

"Not so," he interrupted. "I left you a note."

"You call that an explanation?" she demanded, all the hurt and frustration of the last days finally coming to the surface. "You think after everything we've had together, everything we've been together, you can just waltz out of my life without an explanation, leaving me to pick up the pieces of the charade you forced upon me? What did you think I was going to say to people? 'Oh, by the way, my husband was never my husband and he's gone somewhere, I don't know where'?" She faced him across the felled body of Margery's husband.

"You owe me a hearing, and you owe me an explanation, Rupert."

He just looked at her in silence for a moment; then he gave a half-shrug of resignation. "Maybe so. But not in this wind. Come on, let's get inside." He put an arm around her shoulders and propelled her toward the open kitchen door.

Once inside, he stoked up the range until it blazed, set a kettle on the fire and disappeared into the pantry. He emerged with two bottles and several spice jars. "Sit down by the fire, Diana, you're half-frozen."

For a moment there in the yard, she had thought she had the upper hand, Diana reflected ruefully, sitting in the rocking chair by the range. It had almost seemed as if he was conceding her point. But there was nothing conciliatory in his manner now. She watched him take down two pewter tankards from the Welsh dresser, pour liberal amounts of brandy and rum into each one, add slices of lemon and orange and generous sprinkles of spices. He poured hot water from the kettle onto the concoction, then heated the poker in the range for a moment before plunging it into the contents of each tankard in turn. The mixture sizzled, and the glorious scents of nutmeg and cloves filled the kitchen.

"Here, get that down you." He handed her one of the tankards. "And let's thrash this out once and for all. You've come a long way for whatever it is you want from me."

It seemed as if he was not going to make this easy for her, but Diana was now in so deep, his off-putting manner could not begin to deter her. "I want to know *why* I can't ask a simple question without your cutting me off completely. You were at Mafeking, you carried Jem off the field, but *why* did no one see you there? Can't you understand that my wondering that is not tantamount to accusing you of lying?" She took a tiny sip of the steaming liquid in her tankard. "Answer me that, Rupert." Her voice was low but fierce. One way or another, she was going to get her answers.

Rupert sat astride a kitchen chair, his arms resting along its back, the tankard between his hands. "You have the right to ask," he admitted slowly. "But answer me something first."

"Anything."

"Did you consider for one minute that I had lied to you? That I had not been with Jem?"

"No, I did not think you had lied, but I did wonder what you weren't telling me," Diana replied carefully. "There must have been something."

"Gunpowder," he said. "I wasn't telling you about the gunpowder."

Diana looked quizzical. "So tell me now."

He told her the full story of that half hour in the May dawn, and when he fell silent Diana stared at him. "I don't understand why you refused to tell me that before. You were doing what had to be done and it took you away from Jem's side at a critical moment, but it was the right thing to do . . . the *only* thing to do."

"Yes," he agreed without expression. "It was. But I have never been able to forgive myself for not being beside Jem during the attack. If I had been, things might have been different. He might be here now." He shrugged. "I'll never know, and I have to live with not knowing."

Diana stared into her cooling punch. "I suppose, because you couldn't forgive yourself, you thought everyone else would see it as you do. A betrayal of friendship . . . of brotherhood even."

"Somewhat convoluted reasoning, but yes."

She drank the last of the heady drink and it stiffened her resolve. She looked at Rupert, asking directly, "Why don't you trust me?"

He frowned. "But I do trust you."

"If you did, you wouldn't close yourself off from me when you think I'm asking intrusive questions," she retorted.

A slight smile touched his eyes for the first time since he'd appeared in the yard. "I am a deeply flawed human being, my dear girl. Can you forgive me?"

"You're no more flawed than I am," she declared. "And I give you fair warning, Rupert Lacey, that I shall never hesitate to ask you anything I want to, and if you don't give me a proper answer, I shall withhold my favors. So there." The sparkle was back in her eyes, and it was answered by the gleam in Rupert's.

"Oh, will you indeed?" he murmured. "Well, we shall see about that, madame." He got up and went to the door, throwing the bolt across before turning slowly to face her. He crooked a beckoning finger, and Diana rose to her feet, drawn inch by inch toward him, unable to resist the demand in the green eyes or the imperatively inviting finger. Not that she had any desire to resist, no desire at all.

A long time later, she stirred among the pile of blankets and cushions that made a makeshift love nest in front of the range. She burrowed deeper into the hollow of his shoulder, and his hand moved in a lazy caress down her flank. The nest was wonderfully warm, and the soporific effects of the punch combined with the delicious postcoital languor to render her almost insensible.

She murmured in faint protest as Rupert moved his arm, sliding out from under the covers. He stood up and threw more wood on the range, then, wrapping his nakedness in one of the blankets, he went across to the window looking out onto the yard.

"Is he still there?" Diana mumbled from deep inside the nest.

"No. I daresay the cold woke him up eventually."

Rupert turned back from the window. "Are you hungry?"

Diana considered the question. "I suppose I am," she acknowledged. "But it's so snug in here, I don't want to move." However, she forced herself to sit up, pulling blankets around her as she did so. "Will Margery be all right with that brute? He's bound to be mad as fire."

"She knows how to look after herself," Rupert replied with confidence. "Except when he takes her by surprise, like he must have done this morning. She'll have barred the door to him as soon as she got home, and if that doesn't deter him, she'll run him off with a shotgun."

"A formidable lady," Diana observed.

"That she is." He went into the pantry and emerged almost immediately with a tin. "She also makes a most succulent and sinful lardy cake."

"What's a lardy cake?"

"Oh, a Yorkshire delicacy, one of many." He opened the tin and brought it over to show Diana. "See."

Diana looked doubtfully at the contents of the tin, a glistening cake, studded with swollen raisins and liberally sprinkled with sugar. "Why's it so shiny?"

"That's the lard," he informed her. "Hence lardy cake." He broke off a chunk and lifted it to his lips. "Delicious. There's nothing on earth like it." He broke off another piece. "Here, try it."

"But it's dripping with grease," Diana said in horror. "I can't eat that."

"Don't be so namby pamby," he teased. "Try it, just a taste. You don't know what you're missing."

To humor him, Diana took a minute bite. Sweet, sticky, dripping with lard. She swallowed and shuddered. "You're right, there's nothing on earth like it, and I never want to taste it again."

"You'd be glad of it during lambing season, when you're out on the dales in the winter snow," he told her. "The fat warms the blood."

"What else is there to eat?"

"I saw a couple of pig's trotters in the pantry," he offered. "And a dish of tripe and onions." He laughed at her horrified expression. "Yorkshire folk have a word to describe you soft southerners," he said. "Nesh."

"I may be nesh, but I'm too old to change," Diana declared, hauling herself to her feet. "There must be something palatable in the pantry." She padded barefoot across the kitchen, trailing blankets. "There's a ham, a loaf of bread, butter, cheese and what looks like a chicken pie," she called from the pantry. "Everything necessary for a most respectable picnic."

She emerged into the kitchen with her arms full, setting her treasures on the long table. There was no sign of Rupert. "Where are you?"

"Getting these." Rupert reappeared from a doorway leading to a flight of stairs. He set two dusty wine bottles on the table. "My grandfather put down an excellent cellar."

Diana fetched plates and glasses from the dresser. There was something about this cozy domesticity that felt right, she decided. They made an absurd couple, barefoot and swathed in blankets, but the sense of shared intimacy felt deeper than it had ever done before. She looked at him, wordless, a question in her sloe eyes.

Rupert read the question and nodded slowly. He reached for her hands, drawing her close. Tilting her chin with a long forefinger, he gently kissed her mouth. "All in good time," he said obliquely, then turned aside to pull the cork from a wine bottle. He poured a little into a glass. He inhaled deeply as he swirled the wine in the glass, before nodding his satisfaction and pouring the deep red liquid into both glasses.

He handed her one and said with a half smile, "I can't imagine what possessed you to make this god-forsaken journey, but I am eternally grateful you did, my sweet."

"You know full well why I made it," Diana said. "I wasn't going to let you have the last word."

"I can only applaud your consistency," Rupert responded with a sudden grin that changed his whole expression. "And be grateful for it. Now, let's eat. We'll go back to London tomorrow, if you can face the journey again so soon."

"I don't mean to offend you, but more than one night in this unwelcoming spot is as much as I can stomach," she replied.

"It's better in the summer," he said, sitting at the table, pulling her down to the bench beside him. "The countryside is magnificent."

"We could make the house more welcoming," she said thoughtfully, cutting into the chicken pie. "I mean, if you wanted to spend more time here, in the summer, for instance. I'm sure we could make it pleasant."

"A subject for another time."

Chapter Twenty-Two

Diana awoke at dawn the following morning to find herself alone, still snuggled into the blanket nest in front of the kitchen range. She struggled up onto an elbow and surveyed the kitchen. It was deserted, although a kettle was whistling softly on the glowing range. Her clothes were laid neatly over a kitchen chair, but there was no sign of Rupert's. She was summoning the willpower to leave the warmth of her nest when the door to the yard opened and a frigid gust of wind blew into the room.

Rupert came in with two buckets of water from the pump in the yard. He set them down beside the door and felt gingerly into the deep pockets of his jerkin, bringing out a clutch of large brown eggs. "Good, you're awake," he said cheerfully. He went to the range and lifted the kettle, pouring the contents into an enamel basin. "Washing facilities are somewhat primitive, I'm afraid. This is the best we can do for now." He set the basin on the kitchen table, opened a drawer in the dresser and withdrew an armful of towels.

"I'll manage, thank you." Diana clambered out of the pile of blankets. The kitchen was warm, at least. "How do we get to the train station?" She dipped a cloth in the hot water and pressed her face into it, feeling herself come to life.

"We'll take the pony and trap. One of Margery's lads will drive it back." Rupert was cracking eggs into a basin.

Diana finished her ablutions and dressed rapidly, all the while watching Rupert's efficient preparation of breakfast. She didn't know why his skill among the cooking pots should surprise her. She didn't think anything should surprise her about this man. "Where did you learn to cook?"

"The army," he replied, cutting thick slices from a flitch of bacon. "Nothing fancy, mind you, but enough to keep body and soul together. Toast the bread, will you?" He gestured with his knife to a loaf of bread and two toasting forks. "The butter's softening on the range."

Diana speared two pieces of bread on her toasting fork, while the smell of frying bacon set her juices running. Rupert poured his eggs into a skillet, tossed in a handful of herbs and expertly tilted the skillet, lifting the runny eggs until the bottom was set before finally tossing the mixture and catching it upside down.

"*Omelette fines herbes,*" he declared, sliding his creation onto a large plate. "Sit down and help yourself."

"Something tells me *fines herbes* is not a Yorkshire

recipe," Diana observed, buttering the two pieces of toast before spearing fried bacon onto her plate.

Rupert brought a coffee pot to the table and filled two cups before swinging his legs over the long bench and sitting down.

For a few moments, they ate in appreciative silence, then Diana asked, "What time is the train?"

"Nine o'clock," he answered through a mouthful of omelet. "We should leave in fifteen minutes. We have to get over Buttertubs Pass."

"I remember." Diana bit into her toast. "I can't say I'm looking forward to the journey. It's so long and tedious."

"Maybe it won't be so bad this time," he said.

"I suppose having company might make it go faster," Diana reflected. "But much as I enjoy your company, Rupert, I still don't relish that freezing train."

He gave a noncommittal shrug. "We'll get there when we get there."

Diana frowned. It was unlike Rupert to shrug something off by stating the obvious. He seemed to be perfectly sanguine himself about the prospect of the journey, and he was probably right that it was the only way to deal with it.

A lad of about fourteen stuck his head around the door just as they were finishing. "Ma says as 'ow ye need me t' take you to Hawes, Mr. Rupert, sir."

"Yes, we do, Charlie. We'll be with you in five minutes."

The head disappeared, and Diana got up quickly. "We should clean this up."

"No, leave it for Margery. She'll be here later. Let's go."

"Give me a minute." Diana headed out into the yard, making for the privy, reflecting that one night in this bleak and uncivilized spot was more than enough. She should be thankful the warmth and civilization of Cavendish Square awaited at the end of today's miserable journey.

Rupert was standing beside the trap, tapping his foot in characteristic impatience. "Sorry," she said breathlessly as she hurried across the cobbles. "But there are some imperatives that have to be obeyed."

He handed her up onto the bench without responding and climbed up after her. "I'll take the reins, Charlie." The lad handed them over and climbed into the back. "Wrap this around you. It'll be cold going over the pass." Rupert handed Diana a thick travel rug, much more sanitary than the horse blanket that had warmed her on her previous journey.

She was glad of it over the pass, but the sun was shining, and because this time she was less anxious, she had time to appreciate the magnificent countryside. The mountain peaks in the distance, the patchwork spread of the fields, the elaborately constructed stone walls. Here and there, a church spire rose against a startling blue sky. It felt wild, untamed, despite the evidence of farms and cattle.

When they reached the station, Diana jumped down before Rupert could offer a helping hand and reached up for her valise. "I'll get the tickets," he said, disappearing into the small station hut where Garth was presumably to be found when he was on duty.

Diana stood on the platform, gazing down the narrow track for any sign of an approaching train. There was a level crossing a few hundred yards to the left, and as she watched, a man ran out waving red flags to alert anyone wanting to cross of a coming train. Rupert emerged from the hut, tucking the tickets into his breast pocket just as the shrill sound of a steam whistle broke the morning peace and the train came trundling into view.

It only had two carriages, but Hawes was on a branch line, as Diana knew, so she was not surprised. She *was* surprised, however, at the direction from which it was coming. "That's not ours. It's coming from the south and we want to go south."

"Don't worry." Rupert bundled her into one of the carriages. "It's a single track. There'll be a points switch farther up to send it back around."

"Oh." Diana sat back. What did she know about trains? You got on them and they took you where you wanted to go. And a lot faster than a horse and carriage.

Rupert leaned back, stretching his long legs in front of him with a contented sigh. "I'm going to have a little nap," he said. "If you won't consider it antisocial."

"No, not at all." Diana tried not to sound surprised. She was not in the least sleepy herself, and Rupert was not in the habit of taking naps; in fact, she could never remember him doing so before in her company. He closed his eyes and his breathing settled into an even rhythm as she watched him. A small smile lifted the corners of his mouth, as if he was dreaming of something very pleasant.

His eyes opened the instant the train began to slow after a mere half hour. "I don't remember the train stopping between Kendal and Hawes," Diana said in surprise.

"It depends on the train," he said easily, standing up to lift their bags off the luggage rack. He dropped the window and leaned out to open the door onto a narrow platform that, even more so than Hawes Junction, seemed to be in the middle of nowhere.

Rupert jumped down to the platform and reached up a hand to help Diana down. "We're in the middle of nowhere," she said, looking at the platform sign. "Why is this Firbank Halt and not Kendal?"

"Because this is where we will catch the train to Penrith," he stated, as if it was the most obvious thing in the world.

"Why are we going to Penrith, Rupert?"

"I have my reasons," he returned with a mysterious smile, looking along the line for the sign of an approaching train.

"But what if I don't wish to go to Penrith, wherever it may be?" Diana asked.

"You will, trust me . . . ah, here's the train." The steam whistle heralded the arrival of the train around the bend in the track. Rupert opened a door to one of two carriages. "Up you get." He boosted her up with an intimate hand under her backside, tossed the bags in after her and climbed in. "We will take lunch in Penrith."

"Will we?" she murmured. "Why do I have the feeling I'm being kidnapped?"

"Probably because you are. But as I said, *trust me, Diana.*"

"Oh, I do," she said, shaking her head in resignation. "I'm always up for an adventure, as you know."

He laughed, and Diana thought he seemed remarkably pleased with himself. He opened his portmanteau and withdrew a silver flask, unscrewing the top. "This'll warm you up." He held it out to her.

She took a swig of cognac and felt the warmth course through her. It also made her feel both light-hearted and pleasantly light-headed. "Why are you kidnapping me?"

"You'll discover, all in good time." He took the flask back from her. "Don't have too much of this. This adventure requires you to be fully in control of your senses."

Diana decided she had nothing to lose by letting herself be kidnapped. She wasn't sure there was much she could do about it anyway, as the train steamed steadily through the Yorkshire countryside.

When they descended at Penrith station, Diana looked around for any clue that would tell her where they were going or why. Penrith was much more of a town than a village, and the platform was quite crowded. The bustle was explained when they walked out of the station into the middle of market day in the town. Stalls lined the High Street, and animal pens clustered in the village square, where an auctioneer was selling livestock to well-to-do farmers, whose wives carried loaded baskets from stall to stall, when they weren't selling their own wheels of cheese and blocks of butter.

"This is so different from Hawes and Thwaite," Diana observed.

"Penrith is the main market town for this part of the Dales," Rupert told her. "And don't be deceived by the appearance of poverty among the folks of the Dales. The farmers are substantial folk—*warm* is the adjective Yorkshire folk use to describe the wealthy—but they don't broadcast it. It's all in the land and the livestock."

It was nothing like Kent, Diana thought once again. Nothing delicate and gentle, nothing nesh about these people going about their business. She wondered if perhaps they were here because Rupert thought she should broaden her horizons. It would be just the kind of unilateral decision he would make. Oddly enough, the reflection didn't annoy her.

"The White Hart does a very good luncheon," Rupert now said, steering her with a hand at her waist across the market square to a timbered hostelry. "Our next train leaves at two thirty, so we have just over an hour to eat."

"Next train to where?" Diana tried again.

"Trust me" was all the answer she got. It seemed to be the theme of this strange journey, from its beginning in Cavendish Square to this market town high up in the Dales.

She was content to let Rupert order lunch. "The

brown trout will be fresh from the local stream this morning," he told her.

"Aye, that it is, ma'am. Our Tom caught it but three hours ago," the serving girl told her, beaming. "An' I picked the blackberries for the pie myself. An' there's a good piece o' Wensleydale t' go wi' the pie."

"They certainly know how to eat in Yorkshire," Diana declared some time later, finishing the last of her apple and blackberry pie. "Oh, with the exception of lardy cake and black pudding."

"Both of which I happen to like," Rupert said, reaching into his pocket for his billfold. "But I grew up on them and I daresay that's a prerequisite."

"When you were little, living with your grandfather, who looked after you?" Diana asked, halfexpecting him to snap shut as he had so often in the past at any mention of his childhood.

"Oh, various folk. I lived mostly in the kitchen until I went away to school. The kitchen folk didn't take much notice of me, but they let me hang around by the range, and the cook made sure I was fed."

"Who put you to bed?" Again she waited for the rebuff, but it didn't come.

"I don't really remember. Probably no one." He sounded as if it was a matter of indifference as he rose to his feet, putting money on the table. "Come, we can't afford to miss the next train."

"Why not? We could always stay here," Diana suggested, following him willy-nilly to the street.

"No, we most certainly could not," Rupert declared. "You're being kidnapped, remember?"

"I'm happy to be kidnapped in Penrith," she offered.

"Don't be argumentative, Diana."

"I thought you liked consistency," she said with a grin.

For answer, he seized her hand and pulled her after him to the station.

Their third train of the day was rather larger than the previous two, and the carriages were actually heated with coal-burning stoves. They found themselves sharing a compartment with two women, each carrying covered baskets. Silence seemed to be the order of the day, and Diana was content to have it so. She looked idly out of the window at the passing countryside and wondered where on earth this mad adventure was going to deposit her. Once or twice she glanced at Rupert, but nothing in his calm expression offered a hint. After a few minutes, her eyelids began to droop with the rhythmic clatter of the train on the rails and the warmth of the carriage.

She came awake abruptly when the train steamed to a halt. "Where are we?"

"You'll see." Rupert opened the carriage door and jumped to the platform, holding up his hand to help her down.

Diana stepped down beside him and looked around the small station. They seemed to be the only passengers to alight. And then she saw it.

The sign over the platform read Gretna Green.

She turned her astounded gaze on Rupert, who

was regarding her quizzically. "What . . . what is this, Rupert?"

"I am going to marry you over the anvil," he responded, as calmly as if it were the most obvious thing in the world.

Diana rubbed her eyes as if to dispel some dream. "Aren't you supposed to ask me?"

"I've done that once already, if you remember." His voice was quiet, his gaze fixed upon her face.

Diana swallowed. "Yes . . . yes, I do remember."

"Is it presumptuous of me to assume your answer is the same now as it was then?"

Dumbly, she shook her head.

"Good, then let us go and find the blacksmith." He transferred her valise to the hand that held his portmanteau and took her hand in his free one. "Cat got your tongue?"

Diana found her voice at last. "This is the most . . . most absurd and utterly perfect idea you have ever had, Rupert Lacey."

He grinned at her. "I thought so. Less than a day's journey . . . it seemed to fly in the face of fate to ignore the opportunity."

Diana was still too dumbfounded to say much as they left the station and found themselves in a small, picturesque village, complete with village green, whitewashed cottages and the blacksmith's cottage, boldly proclaiming itself the home of the Marriage Room. Rupert steered Diana across the street and into the building.

"Well, what do we have here?" A woman emerged from a room to one side of the square hall. She regarded the couple shrewdly. "Runaways, are ye?

Don't look much like it. I'd lay odds, m'dear, you're well over marriageable age and don't need no one's permission to get wed."

"Indeed I am, ma'am," Diana said with a tiny laugh. "It's not age that's the problem. It's just a very complicated story, and we would like to be married with a minimum of fuss and a maximum of speed. Can that be done?"

Rupert laughed. "You always had a way with words, my sweet." He turned to the woman. "We need two witnesses, I understand."

"Oh, aye, there's plenty on call. They'll expect a little summat for their trouble."

"That goes without saying," he reassured her. "And who will officiate?"

"Oh, that'll be my Davey. He's done enough of 'em, you've no need to worry."

"Is he the blacksmith?" Diana inquired.

"Oh, bless you, no, my dear. It's been many a year since the blacksmith did the job. No, anyone can do it now, but my Davey's the best. Now, if you'd like to pretty yourself up a bit, I'll show you upstairs. And you, sir, could do with a glass of our finest single malt, I'm guessing. Go you into the parlor for a bit, and I'll send the lad to fetch Davey."

"Oh, Diana," Rupert called her back as she turned to follow her hostess. "You had better give me back the ring so that I can do the job properly when the time comes."

"This is bizarre," Diana said, sliding the ring off her finger. "I can't wait to tell Fenella and Petra."

Rupert merely raised his eyebrows and slipped the ring into his pocket.

Never in her most extravagant dreams could Diana have imagined the wedding she had, standing in a parlor with an elderly gentleman shuffling papers, murmuring various legal phrases like an incantation. Two men, one of whom, judging by his leather apron, was definitely the blacksmith, stood as witnesses, the ring was returned to her finger, papers were presented; and signed, whiskey was drunk to toast the happy couple, Rupert dispensed coins with a lavish hand, and Colonel and Mrs. Lacey walked out onto the main street of Gretna Green.

"Where to now?" Diana asked. "Am I still being kidnapped?"

Rupert smiled. "Only as far as the Black Swan." He gestured across the village green to an old coaching inn. "Where I intend to have my way with my wife."

"Oh, mercy me," Diana murmured, fanning herself with her gloved hand. "What's a poor maiden to do?"

"Exactly what she's told," Rupert responded smartly. "Come, wife of mine."

Epilogue

"Kidnapped?" exclaimed Petra.

"Gretna Green? Really?" asked Fenella.

"Really," Diana affirmed, laughing as she poured champagne for her friends two days later in her parlor in Cavendish Square.

"But that's so romantic," Petra declared, sounding puzzled as she took the glass Diana handed her.

"And Rupert isn't in the least romantic," Fenella said.

"No, exactly." Petra sipped her champagne. "You truly didn't know anything about it, Diana?"

"Truly. And under the circumstances, I don't think it's entirely fair to say Rupert isn't at all romantic." Diana picked up her own glass. "Well," she amended, "perhaps it is. Maybe this was an aberration."

"What was an aberration?" Rupert spoke from the doorway, the dogs bounding ahead of him into the room.

"You being romantic," Diana told him, smiling over her glass.

"Calumny," he returned. "I consider myself very romantic. Is there a glass of that for me?"

"You can share mine." She held out her glass, her eyes laughing at him. It was amazing how different if felt, actually being married rather than pretending to be. They were still going to fight—it was in their natures—but now they could love as openly and vigorously as they could fight.

"It's not just Rupert," Petra pointed out, uncannily tuning into Diana's thought. "You're not in the least romantic either, Diana. That's why you both make such a perfect match."

"I'll drink to that." Fenella raised her glass. "To the most unromantic but perfectly matched couple there ever was."

Rupert held the glass to Diana's lips, then drank himself. "In the spirit of romantic perfection, I am going to be uncivil enough to ask you two ladies to drink your champagne and make yourselves scarce. I find I have some urgent business to discuss with my wife."

"Oh, we know when we're not wanted." Petra drained her glass and set it down. "You haven't even had a honeymoon yet."

"Don't forget they've been married for at least a year, as far as the world's concerned," Fenella reminded her, setting down her own glass. "Lord, is that the time? I'm going to be late."

"Late for what?" Diana inquired. "Anything exciting?"

"No," Fenella replied rather evasively. "Not really. We'll love you and leave you, dearest." She kissed Diana warmly, regarded Rupert with her head on one side for a moment, then reached up and kissed his cheek. "I hope one day someone kidnaps me." She went to the door.

"Oh, I want to be carried away by a knight on a white charger," Petra stated, laughing at her own absurdity. "Goodbye, Rupert." She hugged him with her customary informality and kissed Diana. "Fenella is being very mysterious these days," she confided in a whisper, glancing at their departing friend. "She's always hurrying to an appointment, but she always says it's nothing important."

Diana looked at her husband, who was showing distinct signs of impatience. "We'll unravel it another time," she murmured.

Petra followed her eyes and nodded. "Yes, I see what you mean. Next time, then." She hurried to the door in Fenella's wake.

The door closed, and Rupert drew his wife into his arms, pushing up her chin to kiss her mouth. A knock at the door brought an oath to his lips. "What now? *Yes?*"

Barlow appeared in the doorway. "I'm sorry to disturb you, sir, ma'am, but Mr. Marsden is wondering if you're at home."

"No, we most definitely are not at home," Rupert declared. "Send Mr. Marsden on his way, and for the rest of the day, we will not be at home to anyone. Is that clear, Barlow?"

"Oh, yes, Colonel Lacey. Abundantly clear." Barlow couldn't keep the smile from his lips. "I will ensure you are not disturbed until you ring." He left, quietly closing the door behind him.

"Now," Rupert said. "Where was I?"

Read on for a preview of

Seduce Me With Sapphires

by Jane Feather . . .

available everywhere books are sold
in early 2020!

The Honorable Fenella Grantley turned up the collar of her sable coat against a violent gust of icy wind whistling around the corner of Bloomsbury Square as she turned onto Gower Street. It was a respectable if unfashionable part of London, and one that had become familiar ground in her weekly forays over the last year.

She went up the steps of a narrow terrace house halfway along Gower Street and let herself in through a front door badly in need of repainting. The narrow hallway was equally in need of redecorating, the skirting boards scuffed, the linoleum on the floor scratched and lifting at the edges. The air was chilly despite the rattling huff from a steam radiator, and the gaslight showed only dimly through its dust-coated sconce on the dingy gray wall.

A narrow staircase rose to the upper floor from which the sounds of scales on a piano drifted down. Fenella hurried up the stairs to the first-floor landing.

The piano was louder, coming from behind one of the closed, badly painted doors along the corridor. The chill light of a February morning showed through a grimy window at the far end of the corridor. Fenella opened a door halfway along.

"Good morning, everyone," she greeted the small group of people gathered around a long table in the large room. They were all huddled in coats, gloved fingers fumbling with sheaves of paper in front of them. Another steam radiator grumbled ineffectually from beneath a window, which looked out onto the street.

"Oh good, you're here at last," commented an elderly man with a distinguished mane of silver hair sitting at the head of the table. His threadbare frock coat, fingerless gloves and stringy woolen muffler did nothing to diminish the power of his presence.

Fenella refrained from pointing out that she was actually ten minutes early. "My apologies, Cedric. I didn't realize I was keeping everyone waiting." She offered a general smile, remarking, "It's bitter out there," as she took a spare seat at the table, drawing her coat closer around her.

"It's bitter in here," a young man muttered through his muffler. "If we're to continue meeting like this through the winter, Cedric, we need a kerosene stove or something."

Cedric Hardcastle, an irascible man at the best of times, ran his little acting school out of his run-down Bloomsbury house on a shoestring and glared at the speaker. "If you can pay for the fuel, Robert?"

Robert muttered something and chewed the tip

of a pencil, staring down at the scratched tabletop. Fenella winced. She was the only member of this troupe who could afford to supply both stove and fuel, but she tried not to draw attention to her privileged world. They were all here for one reason: a passion for drama and a longing to tread the boards themselves. Cedric had been a well-known classical actor until alcohol and memory loss had rendered him incapable of taking to the stage, so he'd set up his acting school, the only one of its kind, in the hopes of making some kind of a living. It was a paltry one at best.

Fenella picked up the sheaf of papers in front of her. It was an unfamiliar script; in general, their readings were from various forms of classical drama.

"We're reading a new play today," Cedric announced. "And we're very fortunate to have the playwright with us to interpret any complexities in the script. Edward, do you have anything to say before we start?" He nodded toward the shadows at the far side of the room.

Fenella looked up from the papers, wondering why she hadn't noticed the stranger sitting on the high stool when she'd first entered the room. When he stood up and stepped forward out of the shadows, she wondered even more at her initial failure to notice him. He was a very large man with broad, powerful shoulders and square, competent hands. Fenella had always been drawn to a man's hands. She liked them well-manicured and capable-looking. This Edward's certainly fit that bill. She offered him a curious and friendly smile and was rather put off

to encounter something akin to a scowl. The effect
of the scowl was somewhat diminished by his eyes,
which were of the most penetrating, startling blue
Fenella had ever seen. Thick, unruly black eyebrows
matched the equally untidy thatch of black hair
flopping on his forehead and curling over his collar.
It gave him a rakish air. It was a pity about the scowl,
she thought sardonically.

She glanced down again at the script. *Edward
Tremayne* was written boldly on the title page, and
beneath it, *Sapphire*. The only Tremaynes she knew
socially, the Honorables Carlton and Julia, were the
children of Viscount Pendle, but this morose individ-
ual couldn't possibly be associated with that family.
He reminded her of an ill-tempered, scruffy mongrel,
with his black, overlong hair much in need of a
brush. Which, of course, was most uncharitable of
her, and Fenella was not, in general, uncharitable.

"*Sapphire?*" she queried, pleasantly. "Is that the
title of the play?"

"It's a working title," Edward Tremayne declared
with a dismissive flick of his hand. His voice was deep
and well-modulated. "If you read the script you
might understand the point."

Fenella felt her initial prickle of irritation blossom
into an active dislike. She and Mr. Tremayne were
not going to get along well if matters continued in
this fashion. His arrogance was palpable. But perhaps he was nervous at the prospect of hearing his
play read by strangers, perhaps even for the first
time ever. With an effort, she accepted the charitable
explanation and swallowed her annoyance, removing

her attention from him by deliberately turning her head away and asking Cedric, "Do we have specific parts for the reading, or are we going around the table?"

"You're reading Rose," Edward Tremayne declared. "I don't mind who else reads what. Cedric, you decide."

"Why am I to play this Rose character?" Fenella asked, genuinely puzzled at such a definite statement. "You don't know me. You haven't heard me read. How can you be so sure I'll be right for it?"

"I can't. Call it instinct," he responded.

Fenella frowned, a strange feeling of déjà vu prickling the nape of her neck. There was something familiar about him, a sense she'd caught an image of him in her peripheral vision at some point. A glancing familiarity. She *had* seen him before, she thought. Several times, in fact. She stared at him as the memory crystallized. Once he'd been outside her house, just hovering across the street when she'd come down the front steps. If he hadn't been such a large and imposing figure, she probably wouldn't have noticed him at all among the ambling pedestrians on Albemarle Street. And once, walking down Park Lane, she'd had the unmistakable sensation of being followed. She'd cast an involuntary glance over her shoulder just as a large man disappeared into an alley. Now, the extraordinary thought struck her that perhaps he'd been stalking her.

Ridiculous idea. She was just being fanciful. What possible reason could he have had to follow her?

Anyway, she was far too interested in the idea of
the reading to continue pointless speculation. She
shuffled the pages of the script and quickly saw that
Rose appeared on almost every page. Well, she was
always up for a challenge. This whole acting project
had started as a challenge, one she had kept very
much to herself. Lord and Lady Grantley would
have forty fits if they knew of it; it was hardly a suitable activity for a baron's daughter. For some reason,
she hadn't even confided in her best friends. Fenella
wondered if she was embarrassed or ashamed of this
weird passion, but decided she was neither. It was
just something very personal and private. However,
it occurred to her now that it was definitely time to
confide in Diana and Petra. The secret was getting too
demanding to keep to herself. The whole business
was taking up too much of her time to continue
pretending to herself that it was just a hobby, of no
more significance than Diana and her racehorse or
Petra and her love of dancing.

"Shall we begin?" Cedric said after allocating the
remaining parts around the table.

Fenella, as usual, quickly lost herself in the drama
of the reading. It was one of the things she loved so
much about the activity. But she wasn't sure about
her character. She seemed more a cipher than a
real person and it was hard to get a handle on how
to play her. Once or twice, she became aware of
Edward Tremayne looming behind her. He seemed
even larger on his feet than he had on his stool.
And he made her nervous, which annoyed her
even more.

She stumbled over a line and heard an audible sigh of exasperation behind her. She slapped her hand on the papers in front of her and turned to look over her shoulder. "Could you possibly stand somewhere else, Mr. Tremayne? You're putting me off."

The blue eyes narrowed, and for a second a pop of fire illuminated their sapphire depths. Edward offered a mock bow. "Forgive me, Miss Grantley, I have no intention of disturbing your delicate sensibilities. In my experience, amateur actors can't afford to be too sensitive."

"I am not in the least sensitive *or* delicate," Fenella retorted, wondering what she could have done to arouse such hostility from a stranger. "But when all I can hear is your heavy breathing down the back of my neck, I find it impossible to concentrate." Her gray eyes snapped at him.

He stepped back, raising his hands in a defensive posture. "The lady has a temper, I see. Where should I put myself, ma'am, so that I don't disturb your concentration?"

"I couldn't care less," she stated. "Just don't stand behind me." Fenella was aware of the interested, amused eyes of her companions. This completely unnecessary spat was proving entertaining to everyone but her.

"This *Rose* character has no stuffing to her," she declared, now more than ready to do battle. "She's just flat words on a page. There's no fire, no emotion, no hint of complexity, nothing to work with." She ordered the papers in a neat pile in front of her.

"I have no interest in this reading, Cedric. I apologize to you all." She stood up abruptly, not caring for the moment what bridges she was burning. Drawing on her gloves, she left the room, an astounded silence in her wake.

She marched down the stairs to the sounds of the piano scales repeating endlessly behind her and let herself out onto Gower Street, hugging her anger and frustration to herself against the February cold. She rarely lost her temper; it tended to do no good, more often the opposite, not to mention a loss of dignity, and she was angry with herself now for letting Tremayne's arrogance and contempt provoke her into abandoning an activity that gave her so much satisfaction. She turned the corner toward Bloomsbury Square.

"Hey, hold on a minute, Miss Grantley."

The voice behind her made her increase her speed. She heard his steps coming up fast at her back. "Obviously I didn't make myself clear, Mr. Tremayne. I have no interest in your company and even less in your play." She spoke without slowing, but he caught up with her easily and fell into step beside her. He'd followed her in haste, judging by his unbuttoned coat and gloveless hands.

"Allow me to buy you a cup of coffee, Fenella . . . I may call you Fenella? We have some fences to mend, it would seem."

She stopped and looked up at him, exasperated that she had to look so far up to meet his eye. "No, you may not call me Fenella. And no, I don't wish for coffee. Also I have no interest in mending fences

of any kind. Good day to you, Mr. Tremayne."
Spinning on her booted heel, she stalked off toward
Bloomsbury Square.

She was not completely surprised when he refused
to accept his dismissal and instead drew level with
her again, putting a hand on her arm. "Please, just
listen to me, just for a minute."

His tone was so different from the mocking sarcasm
of earlier that she slowed almost involuntarily, glancing up at him again. Those blue eyes were different,
warm, amused and most definitely penitent. "I was
horrid, I know. Please forgive me. Sometimes, when I'm
particularly anxious about something important, I
can't seem to help myself. I become most unpleasant
to people."

"I see," Fenella said dryly. "And is this unfortunate change of character a frequent occurrence,
Mr. Tremayne?"

He ran a hand through the disordered thatch of
hair, pushing it off his forehead. "I deserve it, I
know. But could we go somewhere warmer while
you excoriate me?" A violent gust of wind whistled
around the corner of Bloomsbury Square, as if in
punctuation.

Fenella felt an absurd urge to laugh. Not for one
minute did she believe the humble penitent side
of Edward Tremayne, but she found herself both
intrigued and amused by it.

"You may buy me a cup of hot chocolate, Mr.
Tremayne. There's a café on the far side of the
square."

He bowed with a flourish. "You do me too much

honor, ma'am." He offered his arm with an air of scrupulous formality.

Fenella slipped her gloved hand inside his arm and, feeling very much as if she was acting a part in some comedy sketch, directed her step to the café in the square.

Connect with U s

Books by Bestselling Author
Fern Michaels